VAMPIRES' SHARED BRIDE

Dark Lords of London

Book 4

JESSIE DONOVAN

Mythical Lake Press, LLC

Vampires' Shared Bride

Mythical Lake Press, LLC

Print Edition

www.JessieDonovan.com

Cover Art by Laura Hoak-Kagey of Mythical Lake Design

ISBN: 9798891561007

A Note About Terms

The majority of this book takes place in 1890, and as a result, some of the words or phrases we use every day in the twenty-first century will be different in the past. Please be aware that using those different terms was done deliberately. (I.e. gaming hell is the phrase that means casino, etc.) I always make it clear through context what those older terms/phrases mean, though. Besides, part of the fun of this series is having future versus past constantly battling it out with one another. I hope you enjoy reading it as much as I did writing it. —JD

Chapter One

Summer 2025
Greater Seattle Area
Washington State, USA

Meadow Vale was lost in the book she was reading when a loud clatter came from the kitchen, and she froze.

Since she lived alone in her one-bedroom apartment and didn't have a boyfriend, her place should be quiet. Especially since she didn't have any pets.

As the last echoes of a pan hitting the floor filtered through the wall, she tossed aside her ereader and went to the door. Pressing her ear to it, she held her breath and listened.

Silence.

And yet, her stomach churned, and her heart raced. After being forced to live in hiding for nearly six years, she was jumpy to begin with. But those years had also taught her to take notice of anything out of the ordinary, especially once her siblings had stopped contacting her nearly three years ago.

Pushing aside the sadness at what might've happened to River and Yesenia, Meadow reached for her baseball bat as she simultaneously gathered her magic. As much as she hated her abilities, she would use them to save her life.

After a few more beats, her powers sensed a pair of males nearby. Her magic itched to reach out and manipulate them, but she held back. For now. Because she didn't want them to try forcing themselves on her. No, if she were patient and concentrated, she might just get them to follow her commands.

Although it wasn't a guarantee.

Not wanting to think about her lack of magical training compared to other fae witches, Meadow breathed evenly and focused as much as she could, given the intruders. Her gathered magic pulsed, waiting, and she tightened her grip on the baseball bat.

After a few more beats, her bedroom door crashed open, and two vampire males rushed into her room.

Since she stood behind the now-open door, they couldn't see her yet. And as they spun around, she drew on her power and directed it at the closest of the two males, letting her magic wrap around him.

He's the one you want. You want each other. You must be together, or you may as well jump out the window.

The first male she'd targeted stilled and faced his companion. His eyes turned heated, and he stalked toward the other.

Then Meadow wove the same spell on the second vampire. Within seconds, they were kissing and lowering to the bed.

Not waiting around to see what happened, she grabbed the small packed bag in the hall she always had at the ready, put on shoes and a jacket, grabbed her purse, and dashed out the door.

Thankfully, it was late at night, so she didn't run into any of her neighbors beyond a few high school kids drinking and smoking weed in a car.

However, they didn't even notice her as she hurried across the parking lot, out of the back gate and into the small woods behind the apartment complex. The ready escape route was yet another reason she'd picked this place, beyond it being cheap.

Then she ran, heedless of the bushes and branches that scraped her skin. All that mattered was getting away from the vampires, the ones who'd been looking for her and her siblings for years.

Ones that might've killed her brother and sister already.

Not now. Think of that later. Meadow kept running until her side hurt, and she looked for some thick underbrush to hide in. Once she managed to squeeze her way inside some ferns and bushes—grateful there weren't any nettles—she drew in deep gulps of air, thinking maybe she should take up running.

You have bigger things to worry about now, don't you? She'd always known that one day either her father or Derrick Yates—a vampire mob boss that her father owed money to—might find her. And yet, after so many years of living under a false name and always looking over her shoulder, she'd thought maybe, just maybe, they would've forgotten about her.

But considering two vampires had just broken into her apartment, the odds weren't looking good. And now? Now, she had no idea what to do. If she went to her mentor, Stacey Green, she would probably put the female in danger.

Which left one option—to run and start over. Again.

For a few beats, her eyes heated with tears. All she wanted was a quiet life, one where she could have a normal job, read books, and never have to use her magic again. The ability to control lust and desire had always been a burden and a curse for her. She couldn't even attempt to date, always afraid she'd let her powers out and the male would want her for the wrong reasons.

And worst of all, her siblings might've died trying to protect her from their father and Derrick Yates.

River, Yesenia, where are you? She'd always held out hope that they'd find her, but after so many years, she wasn't so sure. The pair loved her fiercely and would make contact if they could.

Slumping to the ground, she propped her head on her knees and willed herself not to cry. She needed to plan what to do next, all without endangering the only other person who meant something to her around here —Stacey.

But how?

Tears trickled down her face, and she didn't fight them. While she sobbed silently—she wasn't stupid enough to want to draw attention—she wished she could have a normal life. One full of love and laughter instead of fear and resentment.

But who was she kidding? That wasn't the life for her.

Her sobs quieted, and she turned to lay her cheek on knees and listened to the summer sounds of crickets and some distant frogs.

Just as the sounds started to soothe her, something tugged at her. Before she could look to see if the vampire males had found her, the tugging increased, and the world went black.

Chapter Two

Late September 1890
Nyx's Kingdom Pleasure House
London, UK

Laurence "Laurie" Yates was writing down ideas for the following month's themed rooms and balls when Joseph Hope—his friend and business partner—grunted loudly. After looking up, Laurie blinked. A female sat in Joseph's lap, unconscious, with bits of leaves and twigs in her hair.

Before he could do more than blink, the other male groaned and put a hand to his head. And then took a breath. And another.

It took him a second to recognize what was happening—the female had just blooded his best friend, meaning the female was his fated one.

A thread of sadness and jealousy shot through him, but Laurie pushed it aside. His own feelings didn't matter, but the female appearing out of nowhere meant his sister-in-law, Yesenia, had been using her magic again.

Yesenia was a time-wielder, and had been bringing people from the future to their fated ones in this time period; three in total so far. But they'd all previously landed in her husband's home.

As Joseph closed his eyes and continued to breathe, the female started to slump and tumble off his lap. Laurie rushed over just in time to catch her before she landed on the floor. As her soft body collided with his, he noticed her pointed ears.

But that was the last thought he had before a loud clanging filled his head. Over and over again, getting louder and louder, to the point he wanted to scream. He just barely managed to lay the female on the ground before it became overwhelming, and he felt like he might vomit.

He sucked in a breath, and another, the pain lessening a little as the sound continued to clang inside his mind.

Once he finally didn't feel like his head might explode, it hit him—he was breathing.

The female had blooded him.

After opening his eyes, he met Joseph's dark brown ones, and judging by Joseph's gaze, he understood the same thing—the female had blooded them both.

Meaning the three of them were fated ones.

A thread of joy shot through Laurie as he'd always

wanted to be blooded, and especially with both Joseph and a female. They'd always enjoyed being a threesome the most, back when they could still get hard and have sex.

But before he could say a word to his longtime friend and former lover, the female on the ground groaned, and they both rushed to her side.

Laurie brushed some hair off her face, and despite the leaves and smudges of dirt, he couldn't believe how pretty she was. Full lips, a soft, round face, and while her nose was slightly too long, it added a dash of character.

But as he scanned her face, something niggled at him. Something about her was familiar, and yet he couldn't quite place it.

Joseph finally spoke. "She looks a little like River."

River Vale was the fae witch healer married to Laurie's sister, Nora.

And who had a younger sister named Meadow.

Laurie shook his head. "No, it can't be."

Joseph raised an eyebrow. "Shall we bet on it? Because I'm nearly positive this is Meadow, the youngest Vale sibling."

"The one who controls lust and desire, but hates her powers? That one? Bloody hell, maybe it's true that vampires having fated ones really is a curse put on us by the fae witches centuries ago."

Of all the females to blood them, one who hated lust and desire and sex was the worst possible fit. Because Laurie and Joseph ran a pleasure house where different paranormals—and occasional humans—came to live out sex fantasies or interests or to merely spice things up in their marriages.

Sex and pleasure was their livelihood, and if this was indeed Meadow, she wanted nothing to do with it, according to Yesenia and River.

Joseph reached out and traced the female's cheek, gentle in a way only Laurie and their former shared bed partners had seen. Usually Joseph was quiet and serious to the world. Laurie was one of the few who knew he used it as a shield.

His best friend removed his hand from the female's face and murmured, "Maybe we're the best ones to help her embrace her powers. Have you thought of that?"

Before he could answer, the female groaned, the sound shooting straight to Laurie's cock. But somehow he managed to tame his lust, not wanting to scare her, and had himself under control by the time she fluttered her eyelids open.

"Are you hurt?" Laurie asked.

The female's hazel eyes met his, then darted to his mouth—or more specifically, his fangs—and she screamed as she backed away. Joseph shared a look before the other male stated, "We won't hurt you. I know that's what a villain might say, but it's true. We know River and Yesenia. And if you calm down, we can send for them to come and see you."

The female blinked a second, shook her head, and replied, "No, you're lying. You work with Derrick, I know it." She paused and muttered, "Here we go again," before looking at Laurie.

For one beat, and then another, she merely stared. Then she frowned. "What the hell?" She looked at Joseph, staring again, and then her frown deepened. "I don't understand. Who are you?"

It hit Laurie what she'd been trying to do—use her powers.

He held up his hand and pointed to a ring on his thumb. "Your powers won't work on us, Meadow. Both of us bought these protection rings decades ago."

"Wait, how do you know my name?"

She glanced from Laurie to Joseph, and back again. Joseph answered first, "I'm Joseph, and he's Laurence, although everyone calls him Laurie. We run a pleasure house in London, hence why we have protection rings. We can't risk being manipulated by any fae witch that visits and uses their magic as part of their play."

She blinked. "What is a pleasure house?"

Having spent enough time with River Vale, Laurie knew how to better explain it. "A sex club. After passing a thorough security check, people pay exorbitant fees for a membership to have fun here without judgement. Consensual fun. We don't condone rape or illegal acts here."

Well, mostly for the latter. Humans still had laws against sodomy and other practices, but the paranormals did not. So Laurie and Joseph played by paranormal laws since they were in the vampire territory of London.

It was only then that Laurie noticed the bag strapped across her body. She stood, took out a rectangular object, tapped it, and after about a minute, cursed.

Joseph crossed his arms over his chest and said, "If that's the device River talked about, a cell-you-lar telephone that functions without wires, it won't work here. This is 1890 London. We have telephones, but they're still rare. Telegraphs are far more common."

"Telegraphs?" she echoed. "As in the tapping machine things?"

Laurie resisted a smile, and before Joseph could go into the history of telephones and telegraphs—his friend loved tinkering with electrical objects—he said, "Look out of the window beside you. That'll probably be more helpful than two strangers telling you to believe them."

She kept a close watch on them as she inched closer to the window. After pulling aside the curtain, she glanced out and instantly dropped the fabric. "No way. That's impossible."

"Hmm, let me guess what you saw—carriages pulled by horses, strange dresses, or maybe even the food stalls on the street?" He took in her appearance, namely the brightly colored and oversized trousers covered in…cats? Wait, no, cats reading books? Her shirt was also oversized, but not big enough to hide the shape of her breasts. Her unconfined breasts, at that.

As he stared at her, his heart pounded, and blood rushed south. It'd been so long since he had either a male or female, let alone shared one with Joseph.

Which he could now do since his heart beat again.

Before memories could inspire what he wanted to

do with both this female and Joseph in his bed, his friend spoke up. "Let us send for your siblings. Whilst you wait in the small parlor attached to our office, I can ring for tea and cakes."

Laurie resisted rolling his eyes. Leave it to Joseph to be proper and still have his manners when a female had quite literally appeared out of thin air and had to be scared out of her mind.

After clearing his throat, Laurie said, "I'll send a note to my brother and sister, and they'll bring River and Yesenia without delay. Joseph, stay with her and give her anything she wants."

The other male nodded, and Laurie rushed out of the room, eager to ease Meadow's worries and fears. His instinct to claim her thudded inside him, and would only get worse with time.

Somehow, some way, he and Joseph would need to ease her into this world and convince her they both needed to claim her with fangs and cock.

Otherwise, they'd slowly go mad.

However, they had some time before that happened. So for now, excitement hummed through him. After so many years in his frozen state, wishing and hoping for his fated one, he was eager to get everything started and finally begin the future he'd always wanted.

Joseph Hope watched as Meadow Vale kept her back

to the wall, her eyes darting between the door and himself.

He hoped Laurie didn't take too bloody long. After what had happened with first Yesenia, and then River and Reika, Joseph was familiar with the shock of first arriving in a different time period. At least now there were several others to help convince her of the truth.

He still couldn't believe the female had blooded not only him, but Laurie as well. Part of him worried that too much time had passed since he and Laurie had firmly put their relationship into only being friends and business partners. The fact Meadow had blooded them both meant they would have to claim her, but it wasn't necessarily required for he and Laurie to claim each other as well.

And yet…he hoped they could be close again. Him, Laurie, and a female third had always been his preferred method of enjoying sex. Just imagining the voluptuous female nearby being naked, her softness against his front with Laurie's hard, muscled chest at his back, made blood rush to his cock.

Stop it, Joseph. She's scared out of her wits. In less than a minute, he had his cock under control and tried to think of what to say to the fae witch.

For years, he'd tried so hard to blend into the background. Because while he could be more himself within these walls, not everyone was as understanding and open-minded about his presence. Humans, especially, resented that he hailed from a vampire horde that covered most of Western Africa.

The female's voice brought him back to the present. "Can I have some water? Please?"

He nodded and gestured at the long, decorative bellpull by his desk. "I need to pull that rope over there to call for a maid. Is that okay?"

Her eyes darted to the rope and back to him. She edged closer to the fireplace, no doubt wanting to pick up the fire poker. "I guess so. But if you move any closer to me than that rope, you'll be sorry."

He resisted smiling. Since her powers couldn't affect him as long as he wore his ring, he didn't think she could overpower him, not even with the iron poker. "I won't, I promise."

Doing his best not to make any sudden movements, he walked to the bellpull and tugged. Instead of retreating, he remained where he was. When Meadow didn't inch away, he stated, "You have unusual clothing."

She crossed her arms over her chest, which only plumped up her breasts. Before his mind could dwell on what color her nipples were, she replied, "I'm in my pajamas. Since I had to run away from some vampires trying to kill or kidnap me, I didn't have time to change."

His gaze shot to hers before demanding, "Who was trying to kill or kidnap you?"

Her eyes moved to his mouth and fangs, and she inched away. "No one."

Aware his brusque tone had frightened her, Joseph reined in his anger and asked, "Whoever they were, they won't find you here. Unless there's a time-wielder in your time period, no one except Yesenia will be able to move you again."

"Time-wielder? Yesenia? What are you talking about? My sister doesn't have any magic."

He could hold back and brush off her comment. Joseph, like most vampires, learned early in life how to dance the line between truth and lies since vampires experienced debilitating pain when they lied. However, he didn't want to do it with this female. Truth had worked better with her siblings, after all. He replied, "Yesenia has magic, and she brought not only you, but two others from the future to the past, one of whom is your brother, River."

She wrapped her arms tighter around herself. "No, you're just making stuff up to get me to trust you. Then, when I least expect it, boom, you'll hand me over to Derrick and his lackeys."

Joseph resisted a frown and wondered how he could get her to believe he had no ties to this Derrick person?

Then he decided more truths might help. Maybe. "If I were selfishly trying to gain your trust, it's because you blooded me and Laurie, and we need to claim you, eventually."

She studied him, probably trying to dissect his words and see if he was skirting the truth.

And Joseph let her. Because sometimes, waiting was more effective than more words.

"Tell me plainly I'm your fated one, with no filler words."

"You are my fated one. And Laurie's. You started both of our hearts."

After a few beats, she replied, "So that just means you'll be nice to me until you can claim me, and then you'll look for a female more in your guys' league. Someone you want to parade around half-naked in this place and be the envy of all. Which isn't me, of course."

As happened with others from the future, Joseph didn't understand the meaning of some of her words or phrases. However, he understood the latter part completely. "If you were to ever grace the halls half-naked, Laurie and I would have to fight off most of the males, and quite a few females, who'd want to bed you."

Her eyebrows drew together. "Vampires aren't supposed to be able to lie."

"I'm not. It's the truth. Your voluptuous figure would drive most mad."

Including him, although Joseph did his best to keep his lust in check.

She searched his gaze for a few beats and looked away. "Whatever. I'm too tired to dissect vampire half-truths right now."

He wanted to shout that he wasn't lying. And yet, he sensed she wouldn't believe him.

What had the males in the future done to her?

To avoid getting angry at their neglect and stupidity, Joseph decided to move the conversation back to Meadow's family. "Your sister has been working hard to learn how to use her magic. It's been six or seven months now, I believe, since she started training. Her dedication is admirable, although it's been rather hard on her husband since they're still newly married. He's quite besotted, actually. It's been amusing to watch."

Her gaze shot back to his. "Wait, Yesenia has a husband?" Meadow rubbed her forehead with one hand. "I must be dreaming. I don't know how or why this feels so real, but maybe those vampire guys drugged me before strapping me into a virtual reality machine just to mess with my mind."

Joseph had no idea what the latter was, but before he could ask, Laurie rushed back into the room. "They'll be here as soon as they can." He glanced at Meadow's overwhelmed expression and sighed. "You could've waited to explain some of this to her, Joseph. She just arrived and needs time to take it all in."

"Why? Now she can confirm being in the past, as well as being our fated one, once her siblings arrive."

At the bewilderment in Laurie's gaze, Joseph nodded. Yes, he'd told her.

Thankfully, there was a knock on the door, and the maid entered with a cart carrying water, tea, wine, bread, and some small cakes. Once she left, Joseph motioned toward the cart. "You may as well eat something."

She eyed it dubiously. "For all I know, they're blood-filled cakes. So, ew, no thank you."

Joseph snorted at the same time as Laurie barked out a laugh. The other male spoke first. "Even though we can eat again now that our hearts are beating, I'm waiting to have a nice Yorkshire pudding for my first meal. And Joseph will ask for something disgusting, like jellied eels."

He raised his eyebrows. "They're delicious. They were treats for me as a child."

Laurie shuddered. "You can have them all." He went to the cart, sniffed the wine, and smiled. "But your taste in wine is unmatched, my friend. I'm going to have some. What about you two?"

He nodded, and Meadow merely glanced between the pair of them before muttering, "This is the last time I eat a gummy right before bed."

"Gummy?" Joseph echoed as he took the wineglass from Laurie.

It was hard to focus on her reply since Laurie had deliberately brushed his fingers against Joseph's, but he somehow managed it. "I take them sometimes to calm down, so don't judge me. Because if I get too anxious, I can't control my magic."

She slapped a hand over her mouth and widened her eyes.

Joseph replied, "I still don't know what a gummy is. But stay away from opium. Some use it to relax, but it's addictive and forbidden on the premises."

Laurie frowned at him as if to say, *Stop scaring her.* Joseph shrugged, and Laurie focused on the female. Holding out a glass, he said, "This will calm you down. And whilst you'll want to drink the entire bottle—Joseph is the best at selecting wine, more than anyone, in my opinion—it's not addictive for most. Only to those who need to drink incessantly. If you start doing that, then we'll stop giving you any. At any rate, try it."

Laurie was rambling, which he did to fill the silence when he was unsure of what to say.

Before his friend could scare the female more than with anything Joseph had said, he sipped his glass and sighed at the smooth, tart taste. He'd missed this. As much as vampires enjoyed blood, there was something about a good glass of wine.

After another small sip, he held out the glass to Meadow. "Now you know it's not poisoned."

She hesitated, and so he sipped again. After sighing with pleasure, she finally reached out. "Considering this must be a gummy-hazed dream, what the hell? Let me try it."

He closed the distance and held the glass to her mouth. She tried to grab it, and the urge to take care of her, the female who'd made his heart beat again, was strong.

Not yet. Soon. He relinquished the glass and stepped backward, closer to Laurie.

As she drank, Laurie's hand brushed against his, and awareness rushed through him. Part of him wanted to push Laurie against the wall and kiss him. But they couldn't risk scaring off Meadow. And as he watched her drink greedily, he wanted to kiss her neck and graze his fangs over her skin, all while Laurie did the same to him.

When she finished the wine, she licked a drop of red liquid from her lower lip, and both he and Laurie groaned.

Which was a mistake. Because Meadow retreated to the far side of the room. "I thought you said my magic wouldn't work on you."

Joseph said, "It doesn't. But you're the fated one of

two vampires. Surely you understand what that means?"

Laurie cursed. "I swear, Joseph, you're being entirely too honest right now."

As Meadow looked between them, someone pounded on the door. "Let us in, Laurie and Joseph. Now."

Ah, it seemed Leo Yates, the vampire Dark Lord of London, had arrived.

Chapter Three

Meadow stood on the far side of the room, still trying to digest everything the vampires had told her, when someone pounded on the door and said, "Let us in, Laurie and Joseph. Now."

It was yet another male with a British accent. Why in the world would she dream of so many Brits? Yes, she loved the accents and often watched too many British dramas whenever she was in a reading slump. But everyone speaking with accents in a dream was definitely a first for her.

Laurie crossed the room, unlocked the door, and opened it. A slightly older and taller version of Laurie, with the same dark hair and brown eyes, pushed his way inside. His eyes finally found Meadow's and widened.

But she barely had a chance to take in yet another vampire before a familiar voice asked, "Meadow? Is that really you?"

Yesenia? She searched until she found her older sister. She looked exactly the same, except for the weird shirt and skirt she was wearing.

Could she be real?

"Meadow?"

River pushed his way forward to stand next to Yesenia.

Was this real? Were they actually still alive?

They both opened their arms, and with a sob, Meadow ran across the room into Yesenia's arms. River's then engulfed them both.

As she hugged her sister tighter, tears streamed down her face. Oh, how she wanted this to be real. And yet, her siblings looked as if they hadn't aged a day since the last time she saw them, over three years ago.

So this must be a dream.

Not knowing how long she had before she woke up, she moved an arm so she could do a three-way hug that included her brother.

For the first time in years, she felt a mixture of safety and happiness.

After at least a minute of Yesenia murmuring soothing words and River holding her close, River spoke up. "This isn't a dream, Meadow. I promise."

She leaned back a bit, until she could glance at her older brother. "But isn't that what my dream brother would say, to make me feel better?"

"Maybe. Although we'll convince you, eventually. If Yesenia could do it with me, about being in the past, we both can do it with you, too."

"I want this to be real, and yet I can't believe it."

Yesenia smiled at her before plucking something from Meadow's hair. She held it up. "Why are there leaves in your hair?"

She shook her head. "That doesn't matter right now. You say I'm not dreaming, but how? I don't understand."

"Come," Yesenia said. "Let's sit down in the nearby parlor, and we can answer some of your questions, and you can answer ours, too. Because you look older, Meadow. What year is it for you?"

"2025."

Yesenia closed her eyes, and then a tear trickled down her cheek. "I'm so sorry, Meadow, so very sorry that I couldn't bring you from earlier. I thought I had gotten it right, but it seems I'm not as skilled as I thought I was."

River placed a comforting hand on Yesenia's shoulder. "You did the best you could, Senia. You know it."

The older male who looked like Laurie grunted and put a hand on Yesenia's lower back. "The fact you accomplished as much as you did in such a short time is brilliant, love. She's here now, and that's all that matters."

A female Meadow hadn't noticed at first, who looked a little like two of the males in the room, spoke up. "Come on. I think we all need to sit down, have some tea, and let Meadow ask her questions. I can answer one, though—My name is Nora, and I'm River's wife."

Meadow glanced at River, who shrugged. "It's true.

I'm hitched, and so is Yesenia. The scowling bastard is her husband, Leo. But don't let his exterior fool you—he worships our sister."

Her head spun, trying to take all of it in. Laurie spoke from just behind her. "Let's go to the attached parlor. No one will disturb us, and we can nibble on cakes and tea."

Joseph grunted, also nearby. "And you teased me for ordering the cart in the first place."

"All right, all right, it was a good call. Now, let's go into the parlor since this may take a while. And no, we're not leaving yet, River. I can see you want us to, but Meadow will no doubt have questions for us, too. Besides, we can distract Leo and Nora, if necessary."

Nora snorted. "I won't be the problem. Leo might start barking orders, though."

Leo grunted, but before anyone could say another word, Joseph and Laurie herded them into the attached room and ensured everyone sat down. Meadow's head spun as she took in the four people she didn't know. However, she sat on a sofa between Yesenia and River, and their presence eased a little of her anxiety, enough to keep her magic from spilling out.

And once her siblings each took a hand into their own, she slumped against the cushion behind her. "Is this real? Am I really in the past, with you both married, and me blooding two hot vampires?"

River drawled, "I wouldn't exactly call them hot."

Nora huffed. "That's my brother you're talking about. And Joseph is quite attractive."

The male she'd deduced must be Leo jumped in.

"Enough. Meadow needs a chance to ask some questions. We can tease and bicker and the like later."

Yesenia motioned toward the male. "That's Leo, my husband, and the vampire Dark Lord of London. And yes, they still have lords in this time. I suspect within the next few days, you'll be meeting the fae witch Dark Lord, William Khan, as well. He needs to grant permission for you to stay in the vampire territory."

Dark Lords? Territories? And who knew what else. Meadow's head buzzed with questions, but she had no idea where to start.

However, her brother spoke before she could. "I suspect Khan will want you to spend half the time with me and Nora—we live in the fae witch territory—and half with Yesenia and Leo. At least until you decide what to do about Joseph and Laurie." He moved his gaze to the pair standing near the fireplace. "Who'd better not fucking pressure you to do anything that you don't want to do."

Both of the males merely raised their eyebrows. But it was River's wife—Meadow still couldn't believe her brother was married—who spoke next. "Can we stop with the threats for now? Meadow needs answers, and everyone talking at each other isn't helping." The female, who had one blue eye and one green, smiled at her. "What do you wish to know, Meadow?"

Her heart pounded as she looked around the room, which was full of people wearing strange clothing. "So it's true, then? I'm not dreaming and I'm really in the past?"

Yesenia nodded. "Yes, it's true. I ended up here first, right before I was supposed to marry Derrick Yates. It turned out that I had magic the entire time, but no one knew how to look for it since time-wielding magic is rare."

Her sister then went on to tell the story of blooding Leo, their bargain to help each other and part ways, at least until they'd fallen in love and gotten married.

River's story had started out even worse, and Meadow had cried when she'd learned of him being beaten for months by Derrick Yates' lackeys. However, after he'd blooded Nora, she'd taken care of him. And even though the female vampire had never wanted to marry, she'd ended up falling in love with River, too, and had married him.

By the time both of her siblings had finished, Meadow's head hummed, and not just from the wine, either. Even though there were plenty of emotions to unpack later, and even more questions to ask River and Yesenia when they were alone, she wanted some of the closeness she'd had with her siblings once. And so when they finished their tales and asked what she'd been doing, she focused on something unrelated and blurted, "Wait, so if over three years have passed for me, then that means I'm older than River now, aren't I?"

River blinked. "What the fuck?"

"I'm nearly twenty-seven now."

Something flickered in her older-yet-younger brother's gaze. "Then yes, you're older. So does that mean I can be the spoiled youngest? That would be amazing. You'll have to do whatever I want, then."

"I never asked you to do whatever I wanted!"

River smirked. "As a child, you were a little princess, Em. Don't deny it."

Her brother's nickname for her—given because the first letter of her name was M—made her eyes heat with tears. She whispered, "I've missed you, River. So much. And Yesenia, too."

As her brother pulled her into a hug and Yesenia stroked her hair—which she'd always done when Meadow was little—she closed her eyes. Their love had always grounded her and made her feel safe. And despite everything going on, and how her mind should be reeling from everything she'd learned, being close to her siblings relaxed her, and she slowly drifted off to sleep.

As Laurie watched River hold his sister as she slept, it took everything he had not to take her into his arms and cuddle her close. He'd always yearned to take care of someone, to protect them, and to never let them get hurt. Especially since he hadn't been able to help his sister when she'd needed it most.

When he should've ignored his father's threats and tried to rescue her from being a forced breeder before she entered her frozen state.

Joseph touched his lower back and whispered, "Not yet, Laurie. She needs her family right now."

He looked at his friend. At the understanding in

Joseph's eyes, he asked softly, "Don't you want to protect her, too?"

"Of course. But she's not ready. Not yet."

He knew Joseph was right. And yet, patience when it came to love and feelings and sex wasn't one of Laurie's strong points.

Joseph took his hand, squeezed, and released it. "I'll handle this for us. You trust me, right?" He nodded. "Then let me talk to Leo."

As Joseph went over to him, Nora came over to Laurie, took his hand, and asked, "What are you feeling right now? Everyone is concerned about Meadow, and rightly so, but it's a shock for you, too."

She herded him out of the room, to the adjoining office, shut the door, and quirked an eyebrow in question.

He let out a slow breath. "Yes, it's a shock, but not as big of one as River was for you."

"Maybe, maybe not. You've known Joseph a long time, and I know how much you care about him. But is there room for Meadow as well? Because if not, don't try to woo her, Laurie. She's had a difficult time and deserves better. Plus, I'd rather not have River murder you and toss you into the Thames."

"As if he could." She tilted her head, wanting an honest answer, and he replied, "I feel drawn to her, Nora. Yes, I've always been drawn to Joseph. But as much as I care for him, it's never quite felt complete with just him, like something was missing. I've been the happiest when Joseph and I were also involved with a female as well. Maybe it doesn't make sense to some, but it does to me."

Laurie rarely talked about relationships with his sister, mainly because until River, she'd been traumatized to the point of being a recluse.

Now, however, she was better. It was still strange discussing these sorts of things with her, especially since many paranormals even had trouble understanding those in a relationship with more than one other person.

Although he drew the line at telling his sister that the closest he'd felt to being whole and content had been an intense sexual relationship between him, Joseph, and a female vampire.

But even then, something had been missing. And after seeing his siblings find their fated ones, he now knew that he'd never loved their year-long partner. He'd been fond of her, yes. But he hadn't loved her.

Would he be able to love Meadow? And would his feelings for Joseph rekindle as well, despite how long they'd been only friends? Attraction was one thing, but love was something else entirely.

Nora patted his shoulder, bringing him out of his head as she said, "Yes, I think I understand what you're saying. When I was still a girl, before all the awful stuff Father made me do, my best friend had two fathers and a mother. Drusilla, if you remember? The three of them loved each other equally, no less for one or the other, so I know it's possible. But only you can decide if that's the life for you. Fated ones are supposed to be a good bet, but not a guarantee. It'll take work, and sometimes you're not the most patient of people."

"I'm well aware of my faults, Nora. But whilst I'm not 100 percent certain of anything, I know I want to try. Because if I don't, I know I'll regret it forever."

His sister smiled. "Good. Then I'll help you in any way that I can when Meadow stays with me and River. Because you know that whenever the female stays with Leo and Yesenia, our brother will be overly protective. And whilst River might try the same, I can distract him if you and Joseph want some time alone with her."

He hugged Nora. "Thank you." He released her. "But before any of that can happen, she'll not only need to accept she's in this time but also get some kind of magical object from the fae witches that will contain her powers when she wears it. She's afraid of her magic and gets anxious. And if any male besides me or Joseph touches her with lust in his eyes, I'll have to punch him. Females I'll have to settle for shoving away, as I won't hit them."

Their father had beaten them and their mother, and Laurie had vowed to never do that to any female.

Nora shook her head. "You're sounding growly already. But try not to kill anyone, Laurie. Not only will that scare her, Leo will have to punish you or he'll be seen as weak. And right now, he can't afford that."

Mainly because some French vampires—who held a long-term grudge against all British vampires and shifters—were out to get Leo and possibly kill him.

"I won't kill anyone unless it's absolutely necessary,

Nora. But the need to claim Meadow already pulses inside me, and it'll probably only get worse."

She patted his cheek. "You're stronger than you think, Laurie. Draw on that and be patient. Maybe release some tension with Joseph first, and, er, that will help clear your mind."

The fact that his sister could even suggest such a thing to him was a miracle in and of itself, given her past. "River's corrupted you."

She smiled. "A little. But speaking of which, we should probably head back inside and make sure River and Leo aren't butting heads over what's best for Meadow."

And as they entered the room, Laurie's eyes found Joseph's. At the flare of heat there, he knew he might just have to take up his sister's suggestion of releasing tension with Joseph. Maybe then they could both focus enough to figure out the best way to woo Meadow Vale.

Well, provided Joseph wanted the same future as him. If he didn't, Laurie wasn't quite sure what he'd do.

But he'd worry about that when the time came. For now, he needed to tackle one task at a time and try to be patient. It wasn't his strong suit, but he was going to try his best not to bollocks up this chance with his fated ones.

Chapter Four

Joseph, along with Nora and Yesenia, had acted as peacemakers between Leo and River. The two males butted heads a lot, and both had been convinced they knew what was best for Meadow.

In the end, Yesenia had convinced Leo to allow Nora and River to take Meadow to their house. She would need to meet Dark Lord Khan anyway, and being around other fae witches would be less intimidating. Especially given the former hatred and tension between the vampires and fae witches in London.

Even if that past was barely a thought inside the walls of Nyx's Kingdom—there were all sorts of pairings inside the pleasure house—it was a different story in many parts of London's vampire territory. Only Yesenia, who was Leo's bride, could walk freely without fear of any retaliation.

Well, at least from those living in London under

Leo's rule. The French vampires were another problem, and one he and Laurie would have to worry about too since the frogs seemed to target anyone close to Leo, meaning they might go after Laurie and his fated one.

But as Joseph poured another glass of wine and sipped, he pushed aside his worries about enemies and danger. He could strategize about what to do tomorrow. Because tonight, well, tonight he waited for Laurie to return from showing the others out. Would his former lover turned friend want to be lovers again?

His heart pounded as his cock turned harder. It'd been so long, decades, since he'd been able to have sex. When a vampire entered their frozen state, their heart stopped beating. And without blood, a male couldn't harden, let alone orgasm.

And even though he'd managed to survive decades as Laurie's friend and business partner, he didn't want that any longer. Yes, he felt a pull toward Meadow as well, and he wouldn't feel complete until he had them both. But Meadow would take time to woo, and Joseph wanted—no, needed—to fuck and be fucked by Laurie first. Otherwise, he'd never be able to focus and help rein in Laurie's patience to win over Meadow.

Because unlike in the past when it'd been easy to find a third partner to join them, Meadow was more complicated. And not just because her entire world had shifted by being brought into the past. No, he and Laurie needed to help the female learn to embrace her magic. After all, they'd worked with a few fae witches over the years with the same ability to control lust and desire. It often allowed someone to embrace their deepest desires, ones they kept hidden from the world, and fully be themselves. If Meadow could see that, and see how much joy and confidence it brought someone, she might see her powers differently.

The office door opened, and Laurie walked in, shutting the door behind him. Joseph sipped his wine, watching the male he'd known for so many decades. One who was less serious and more spontaneous, but also caring, loving, and softer than a lot of males he'd known over the years.

And damn, how he'd missed being closer to him.

After draining his glass and putting it on the side table, Joseph strode toward Laurie. He stopped about six inches away, and they stared at one another for a second, and another, making Joseph's heart beat even faster.

Then something snapped inside of him, and he reached over and pulled Laurie's head to his and kissed him.

It wasn't soft, but rather hard and demanding. Laurie didn't hesitate to open his mouth, pulling Joseph closer, and their tongues battled as they rubbed against each other.

As he continued to devour Laurie's sweet mouth, he moved his hands and fumbled with Laurie's trousers. Within a few seconds, he opened them and reached inside to stroke his cock. Laurie moaned into his mouth and then caressed Joseph's cock through his trousers.

Pleasure shot through him, but it wasn't enough. Not nearly enough.

He broke the kiss. "I want you naked. Now."

Laurie nipped his bottom lip before growling, "You, too."

They each shed their clothes in record time before pulling each other close and kissing again. Joseph reached down to hold their dicks together and stroked. The feel of Laurie's hard dick against his felt good, so good.

But he wanted more. He needed more.

As if reading his mind, Laurie gentled the kiss and then licked his way down Joseph's neck, teasing his skin with a fang along the way. He groaned and threaded his fingers through Laurie's hair. "Don't stop. Don't you bloody stop."

Laurie chuckled, his hot breath dancing against his skin. "Never again."

After a few more kisses against his neck, Laurie knelt in front of him and took hold of his cock. His eyes met Joseph's, full of heat and longing, and he said, "Watch me. Don't you dare look away."

Then he licked the tip of his cock, and Joseph groaned. Each little flick against his sensitive head made him even hotter, and then Laurie sucked him deep inside his mouth.

Never taking his gaze from Joseph's, Laurie used his hand and mouth to suck and squeeze and tug, the tension building.

It'd been too long, too bloody long, and he wasn't going to last.

Then Laurie fondled Joseph's bollocks as he grazed his cock with a fang, and pleasure exploded. He came in long, intense jerks, to the point he had to lean his hands on the desk behind him to stay upright. The entire time he maintained eye contact, moaning even more as Laurie lapped at his blood and swallowed him down.

Eventually Laurie gentled his mouth and tongue before releasing Joseph's dick, licked the graze closed, and stood. Laurie slowly ran his hands up Joseph's chest until he could pull his head down and kiss him again. They took their time, although Laurie's hardness against his belly told him they weren't done. He murmured, "Your turn, Laurie. I want you inside me."

He smiled slowly, the grin making Joseph's heart beat fast again at how handsome he was.

Laurie replied, "Then it's a good thing that I picked up what we needed on the way. Because, fuck, Joseph. I need to feel your tight arsehole around my cock."

After kissing Laurie slowly for a few more seconds, Joseph turned toward the desk, leaned over, and widened his stance. "Then take me, Laurie. I'm all yours."

Laurie ran his hand over Joseph's muscled arse cheeks. His heart still thumped from tasting Joseph's blood after all these years, but his cock throbbed. Having Joseph's dick in his mouth and driving the male wild had been just as good as he remembered.

But now, oh now, he wanted to stake his claim in another way.

He quickly went to his discarded trousers, took out

the small jar he'd grabbed, and opened it as he returned to Joseph's gorgeous backside. After dipping his thumb into the special recipe they sold at the pleasure house, he teased Joseph's puckered rosebud. Watching the male squirm and raise his hips only made Laurie harder.

Not yet. He wanted to tease Joseph a little first, and so after dipping his forefinger into the jar, he pressed against Joseph's entrance, making him groan, and Laurie slowly fucked him with his finger. And when he added a second one, Laurie also reached down to massage Joseph's balls.

Watching the usually stoic, level-headed male arch up to his touch, all but begging for more, Laurie increased his tempo until he finally pulled his fingers away. After wiping them on the handkerchief he'd grabbed, Laurie caressed one of Joseph's arsecheeks as he liberally covered his cock in the slick concoction.

Then he positioned his cock and pushed, slowly at first, groaning when he finally felt Joseph's tight grip on him. Then using patience he didn't think he had, he rocked slowly and shallowly, caressing Joseph's back and shoulders as he did it. "Ready for more?"

He arched. "Fuck, yes. Stop teasing me, Laurie."

As Laurie picked up his pace and drove deeper, he gripped Joseph's hips and soon he was thrusting hard, savoring how fucking tight he was, and struggled not to come right away.

Then Joseph clenched around him, and Laurie let go, fucking him harder, until the pressure was so great he couldn't hold back. He stilled as his orgasm crashed over him, each jet of his dick almost too intense.

When he finally stilled, Laurie leaned over and wrapped his arms around Joseph before laying his cheek against his back. They both breathed heavily, but as he listened to Joseph's heartbeat beneath his ear, some of the tension he'd been carrying since he'd entered his frozen state eased.

He whispered, "I've missed this. I missed you."

"Me, too."

After a few more beats, Laurie pulled out, cleaned them both up, and Joseph turned to face him. The other male pulled him against his chest, held him, and caressed his back and shoulders. Laurie was a little shorter, and so his head naturally rested on Joseph's shoulder. They stayed like that for a few minutes, merely holding each other, and Laurie's eyes prickled. He couldn't help saying again, "I've missed you. And that was bloody amazing. And yet…"

Joseph rubbed circles on his back. "And yet, it's not quite enough."

Laurie pulled back and searched Joseph's gorgeous brown eyes. "No. I've loved you for a long time, Joseph, and I always will. But I have so much love to give, and whilst it's early, I sense Meadow needs more love than one person can give. Only then will she have the confidence to embrace and discover herself, and become the fae witch she was always meant to be."

Joseph caressed his jaw and smiled. "That's why she has us. We are what she needs, just as we need each other as well as her."

He searched Joseph's gaze. "So you feel the same as me? You're not resentful of me wanting more? Because it's not you, Joseph. You're my best friend, the best male lover I've ever had, and you mean so much to me."

"I know." He hesitated, and then kissed Laurie gently before adding, "I've loved you for a long, long time, Laurie. But as vampires, we're taught to be cautious until after our frozen state ends. And so I always held back a little and thought it safer to never tell you my true feelings."

Laurie smiled. "Unlike me, who bared my heart not long after we met."

After cupping his face, Joseph replied, "Your ability to share your feelings so freely is part of what made me fall for you. It's harder for me, for so many reasons. But as soon as Meadow blooded you as well, joy bloomed in my chest." He laid his forehead against Laurie's. "But if we're to fill the empty place inside both of us, where Meadow should fit, we need a plan."

Laurie chuckled. "Do you already have a ten-point one ready to go?"

Joseph smacked his bum. "No. From here on out, we plan together, discuss together, and introduce Meadow to our world together. Because if we can't win her, we'll never fill the missing pieces of our hearts."

Laurie lifted his head and nodded. "The first step is to determine what Meadow needs the most to feel more at home in this time. Once she's a little more comfortable, then we can think about her powers and the pleasure house and all the rest."

"Well, Nora said we could visit tomorrow afternoon. I wish we could plan it all out now, but in the beginning, we're going to have to rely on your skills to improvise."

Laurie winked. "Making it up as I go along is my specialty." He sobered a fraction before asking, "Will you sleep with me tonight, Joseph? I miss having your heat and chest at my back."

"Of course. But mostly to sleep because between now and tomorrow afternoon, we have a lot to do. If we can delegate more of the pleasure house duties to those we trust, we'll have more time to spend with Meadow."

Laurie stuck out his tongue. "That's no fun."

Joseph's lips twitched. "We'll see. Maybe you can change my mind." He took his hand. "Now, come on. Let's take a bath and figure out what duties we can temporarily entrust to others."

And as Joseph joined Laurie in the tub, he managed to keep Laurie focused enough to discuss who to promote, which employees could be put in charge of upcoming events, and a million other details.

Although as he fell asleep in Joseph's arms, Laurie felt a little more whole. Not quite complete, as he dreamed of holding Meadow as Joseph held him, but he was getting closer to the dream of having love and maybe even the family he'd always wanted.

Chapter Five

The next morning, as Meadow lay in her bed and stared at the ceiling, it really hit her what blooding two vampires meant.

She would have to sleep with them both. And judging from the looks she'd seen pass between Laurie and Joseph, they also wanted each other.

Between her powers and her love of romance novels, the idea didn't really shock her. After all, her favorite stories had almost always been the ones with multiple partners. Not usually the five guys all fawning over one female, though. She loved the intimacy of multiple people loving each other, making memories together, and having more than one person at their back. Always.

But those had been fictional stories, and none of the female characters had ever worried about their powers leaking out and making some male want her against their will.

Although wasn't that what vampires experienced with fated ones, in a way? Wanting someone with no choice in the matter?

All because a fae witch had cursed the vampires long ago, after one of them had broken her heart. Or, so the story went. Originally, she'd doomed them to an eternal frozen life, one without pleasure or the ability to procreate. However, right before the fae witch had died, the vampire who'd broken her heart returned and won her love again. And while the curse couldn't be reversed—she'd been too sick and frail to gather enough magic to do so—the fae witch had softened it by having fated ones start their hearts again and give them a chance at love and a fuller life.

Meadow had always just assumed it was a made-up story, one to make the fae witches look amazing and powerful, and the vampires helpless against their magic. But maybe there was more truth to it than she'd thought.

Someone knocked, bringing her back to the present. And after sitting up in bed and tugging up the covers, she said, "Come in."

River's wife, Nora, entered, carrying a tray. She came over to the bed, settled it over Meadow's lap, and said, "Good morning. Did you manage to sleep at all?"

Unlike her brother, Meadow wasn't as outgoing or easy with new people. Although she was making an effort with Nora, since she seemed like a genuinely nice person. So after a second, she nodded. "A little."

"Well, that's a start. I know it's going to be

confusing, but your siblings and mine are here to help you." She hesitated and then added, "I thought maybe I could take you shopping today for some new things. My maid and I did our best to alter a skirt and shirt, but you're shorter than me, and you should have some properly fitted clothing."

Ah, Nora was being polite about her size. "I'm sure we can sew two skirts together and maybe it'll fit me then."

Nora frowned. "What are you talking about?"

"Never mind. Does River have enough money to help me out until I can figure out something for myself? Because I can work, if I have to. Yesenia temporarily lent me her training bracelet and promised to get me a permanent one soon."

When a fae witch wore a magic training bracelet, it contained their powers. And even now, she lightly traced the engraved symbols on the outside, reminding her that she was safe temporarily.

Meadow hadn't been able to afford one back in the US, and she struggled to accept it would keep her magic at bay. But it was worth a shot, for sure. Maybe going out would truly test it and convince her it worked.

Nora studied her for a few seconds before saying, "Forgive me for being impertinent, but shouldn't you have finished your magic training by now? Or do I have that wrong?"

Meadow sighed. "No, you're not wrong." The vampire merely tilted her head, and something about her gaze told Meadow she could confide in this female. Maybe Nora would tell River, but Meadow would have to talk to her brother about all of this, anyway. So, she continued, "I had a magic mentor, kind of like a teacher, for nearly eight years, but she was never trained to teach others. Despite her best efforts, my powers still leak out, especially when I'm anxious. And I'm always anxious when using magic, so it's a struggle to control anything."

"But you're fine right now. And last night, too."

She pointed to the bracelet. "This will keep it in check. Even if I didn't have it, my powers won't work on anyone related to me. Something about the DNA being too close to manipulate, which is a good thing because, ew, incest. But my magic might affect you if I'm not careful." Meadow tugged the covers tighter around herself. "So if the bracelet ever comes off, you should probably stay far, far away from me."

"I should be safe for the next little while." Nora placed her hand over her lower belly. "I'm carrying River's child, so that means it shouldn't work on me, either, right?"

Meadow stared at her sister-in-law's stomach. "What? You and River are having a baby?"

"Yes. He or she should be here in about four months' time."

Just when Meadow thought she'd heard all the bombshells, another one dropped into her lap. She was going to be an aunt. River, of all people, was going to be the first of them to have a child.

Of course she wanted her brother happy. And Yesenia, too. And yet…

Well, she was a little jealous. Meadow had never even had a real boyfriend, and now her siblings were happy and starting their new adventures, all within a few months of each other. Months that had been long and lonely years for her.

But you blooded two vampires. Maybe there's a chance things will work out, right?

Who was she fooling? Of course it wouldn't work out. What male, let alone two, would want a wife who could accidentally make a room lust after her in the blink of an eye?

Nora placed a hand on Meadow's shoulder and waited until she met her gaze. Then the female vampire said, "I can't read minds, but I see the sadness and defeat in your eyes, Meadow. However, you blooded Laurie and Joseph, and they're not simply going to walk away because you have a few faults. We all have them, after all."

"Maybe, but mine have basically turned me into a recluse with no friends."

After searching her gaze, Nora stated, "I rarely left my brother Leo's house for several decades. I was terrified to do so."

She blinked. "What?"

"It's true. I won't tell you what my father made me do, but it was bad enough that nearly every vampire labeled me a dirty whore. So, I stayed inside where it was safe and predictable, and thought I always would. Until River."

Meadow burned to ask more questions, but didn't want to upset someone she'd only met the day before. So she merely said, "I'm glad my brother could help. River is a wonderful guy, no matter how tough he acts or looks on the outside. He used to read bedtime stories to me when we were little, especially right after our mother died." She smiled. "He'll make a good dad, I just know it."

"I think so, too. But you won't distract me that easily, Meadow. Back to me staying inside for so long, and well, I was probably even more of a recluse than you ever were. And even though I'd given up hope for a different life, I still found love when I least expected it, all because of my fated lord. I want to believe Laurie and Joseph will do the same for you."

Before she could stop herself, she blurted, "Were they together before?"

"I think so. Although back when their hearts were still beating, I wasn't as close to Laurie as I am now, so I don't know the details. However, before you think you'll be intruding, the only relationship that ever truly made my brother happy was with Joseph and another female." She paused, and then asked, "Would you be able to give both Laurie and Joseph a chance? Is that something you'd even want?"

Nora was probably only asking because she didn't want her brother going insane, if Meadow didn't agree to the claiming.

However, she wasn't going to get anyone's hopes up. Because maybe Nora had conquered her problems and was now living her best life. However, Meadow's worries involved magic. And unless she learned how to contain and control it, she would never truly overcome her fears.

But it wasn't as if fae witches could just turn off their powers. Some magically infused objects could dampen it for a while, but never releasing magic had its own problems. Probably similar to a vampire never claiming their fated one or not drinking blood.

She sighed and rubbed her face with her hands. She'd made a tolerable life before, working to stir desire for married couples or at swinger parties, and then going home to her books and crochet and plants. But she had a feeling that her siblings wouldn't leave her alone in this time period.

What was she going to do?

Nora's voice brought her back to the present. "Does your magic work on animals, too?"

Lowering her hands, Meadow frowned at the non sequitur. "Um, no. Just humans and paranormals."

She smiled. "Good. Because an outdoor cat I rescued recently just had kittens and maybe you should have a pair. That way, no matter what you decide, you can have something to cuddle and hold close. It's something I wish I would've thought of during all those years of self-isolation."

"Kittens? I'm surprised River doesn't want to keep them all. He loved rescuing animals as a kid."

Nora murmured, "My son did as well." Before Meadow could ask what she meant, Nora stood and continued, "I'll gather the clothes we've altered for you whilst you take a bath, and then we'll go shopping. And don't worry about the costs—it's our gift to you."

Meadow hated to be further indebted to her siblings and their spouses, but everything she owned was back in the 21st century. "Thank you."

Nora waved a hand in dismissal. "We're family now, and we take care of each other. Although we'll have to take one of Leo's guards with us, who has been posing as a footman, just in case. Unfortunately, my family has some enemies, and we have to be careful."

"I've spent the last six years living in hiding, so I know how to be careful."

Nora looked as if she wanted to reach out and hug Meadow, but hung back. For some reason, she wished her sister-in-law wouldn't.

And yet, it was probably for the best, just in case Meadow's powers got out of control after she had her baby.

"I'm sorry, Meadow. I can't imagine how difficult it was for you, especially during the three years of silence from your siblings."

Not wanting to cry—which she probably would do if she talked about it—she replied quickly, "Well, my motto has become to take things as they come. So, now I need to focus on learning about this time period. Although I'm surprised River isn't here, demanding to take us with twenty guards or something."

"Oh, he probably would try, except for two reasons. One, he has a very special patient that he has to attend to today, and two, you're under Dark Lord Khan's protection until he meets with you this afternoon and decides your fate. Few want to betray him, given his powers and connections."

"So I'll meet with him today, then? Should I be worried?"

"Yes, he's coming here to meet you. Whilst he's a little intimidating, I've seen how he takes care of his people and treats them fairly. I don't think you have anything to worry about, but I can answer more of your questions whilst out shopping. We really need to leave soon if we're to go out at all, so let me get things ready and I'll be back in half an hour."

After Meadow nodded, Nora left. She leaned her head back against the pillow, took a deep breath, and worked on her breathing exercises. Because if she was going to be out among people, she needed to calm down as much as possible and be ready to flee if either she lost her bracelet or someone stole it.

Maybe she shouldn't go.

And yet, she hadn't been able to see much of anything in the dark last night. And as much as she trusted her siblings, it was almost as if she needed to walk around and prove to herself this was 1890.

Once she was as calm as she could be, Meadow went to the attached bathroom and ran a bath. Her brother had insisted on installing hot water, electric lights, and flushing toilets. Thank goodness, because Meadow didn't want to squat over a pot.

As she soaked in the tub, she relaxed a little more and was nearly asleep when Nora and the maid returned. Before she knew it, she was dressed in a long skirt and a shirt with ruffles down the front and giant, puffy sleeves.

Which only made her look even bigger than she already was.

With a sigh, she pushed aside how ridiculous she must look and forced herself to follow Nora. It was time to go out into the world and take in her new reality.

Chapter Six

Grace Black sat inside Dr. River Vale's examination room and plucked at her skirts.

After a lot of delays, today was the day he would magically repair her eyes, which should allow her to see for the first time in her life.

Oh, Dr. Vale had made it clear that she might only see vague shapes in dim lighting, and that she'd have to wear darkened glasses in sunny weather or risk damaging her eyes. And maybe to those with sight, they'd still pity her.

However, Grace had been born blind, had never really understood seeing something or creating a picture, or even what a color was supposed to be. To be able to notice something without a sound or scent or temperature would be brilliant to her.

Not to mention it would give her yet another way to be on alert for danger.

Her older brother, Everett, was the shifter Dark

Lord of London. And he'd finally relented and told her about the French vampires and how they might go after him, especially through her, to get revenge for the past.

While her brother hadn't fought in the Napoleonic Wars—he hadn't even been born yet—a lot of British shifters had. And since they'd helped the British vampires kill most of the French female vampires, as part of a war tactic, it had left many male French vampires unable to find their fated ones. And the longer a vampire's heart didn't beat, the greater the risk of insanity.

Which made them extremely dangerous, but especially for someone like her.

While Everett had never called her a liability, Grace knew she was one. In recent years, it had become fashionable for rich and powerful humans to "own" a shifter and dose them with opium to make them compliant. Those like Grace, who couldn't see, or those who couldn't hear, were the easiest targets.

Her brother had kept her safe in the Scottish Highlands for years. But now, with the French vampires on English soil and looking for revenge? They'd forced Everett to bring her to London to keep a closer eye on her.

And the city was too much for her, in so many ways.

It was too loud, had too many smells, and she couldn't even judge the time of day by the warmth of the sun. Everett had explained that since many households still used coal to cook and heat their homes, the smoke blocked out the sun sometimes.

Longing crashed over her, and Grace missed her home in the wilds of Scotland. And yet, as much as she yearned for cleaner air and less noise, she would never find her fated one back home. None of the males in the nearby villages had stirred her inner wolf, and whilst her metabolism had slowed down to give her time to find her fated one, she would eventually get old.

And both female and beast wanted more out of life. To maybe even be a mother, or at least a wife, and run her own household. Because as much as she loved her older brother, he could be a wee bit overprotective at times.

Before she could castigate herself over thinking unkind thoughts about Everett, there was a knock on the door before the knob turned, and someone stepped inside.

Dr. River Vale's voice filled her ears. "Hello, Grace. Ready for the big day?"

He shut the door and walked closer as she said, "Aye, Dr. Vale. I'm a wee bit nervous, but more than ready."

"And you understand that you'll have to spend the night in our patient guest room, right? Nothing should go wrong, but if I need to adjust my treatment, or you just need time to get used to the changes, I want to be available to help."

"Aye, I know. I had to convince my brother, and that was no easy feat, but he eventually agreed."

"I can only imagine," he drawled. "But Black only wants what's best for you. I'm an older brother, too, and my younger sister arrived here yesterday, so I get it better than most."

Grace frowned. "Your other sister is here in this time too?"

She knew River was from the future, and that his older sister, Yesenia, was a time-wielder. But their younger sister had still been in the future, the last she'd heard.

"Meadow is her name, and yes. But my wife is with her, and I didn't want to delay your treatment yet again, Grace."

"If she needs you, then I would understand."

"No, it's unfair to you. And I would trust Nora with my life. Now, let me quickly check your vital signs, and if everything looks good, we'll get started. Sound okay?"

She nodded, and River said, "I'm going to place my hands on your forehead and the side of your neck, first."

She felt his warm hands, and within seconds, the greater warmth of his magic rushed through her. Soon after, he removed his hands and said, "Everything looks great. First, I'm going to put a set of dark glasses on you. These will be completely blacked out, so I can better control the lighting and test your sight. I know you're eager to see something, but bright light will pain your eyes, Grace. For the first time in your life, you're going to have to worry about stuff like that."

"I know, but I'm ready for it, I promise."

"Then let me put these on."

She felt something perch on her nose and rest on

her ears. The glasses also lightly pressed against her face, surrounding her eyes.

Dr. Vale moved something as it scratched against the floor, and she felt a burst of air as he probably sat down.

He spoke again. "If at any time you feel pain or want me to stop, speak up or raise your hand. Understand?"

"Aye," she stated as firmly as she could. Her heart thudded, and no doubt Dr. Vale could tell, but she didn't want to leave any room for doubt.

"Alright, Grace, then I'm going to place my hands on your face and begin."

His warm fingers pressed against either side of her temples, and she took long, deep breaths. Soon his magic flowed through her, warm and not unpleasant, although soon she felt slight pinches behind her eyes.

"I'm going to repair what I can, and it might hurt a little, but speak up if it becomes too much. I'll do my best to dull it, but every person's pain tolerance is different. Promise you'll signal if I need to add a little magic to ease it."

"I will."

"Okay, then it's time to get to work."

The pressure in her eyes grew, bit by bit, but she merely clutched her skirt and willed herself to keep still. The fact Dr. Vale could do any of this, relying on his knowledge from the future, was extraordinary, and Grace wouldn't take this chance for granted, no matter how intense the pain.

Eventually, it receded slowly, leaving a dull throbbing behind her eyes.

She had no idea how long it was before Dr. Vale removed his hands and spoke up again. "I think that's done. Now, let me turn off the electric light. For the initial test, we're going to use only a single candle."

Even though she heard him moving about, Grace barely noticed it. Exhaustion settled over her, and she struggled to sit upright.

However, she drew on her inner wolf and allowed her strength to keep her awake and somewhat focused.

Eventually, Dr. Vale's voice was in front of her again. "Close your eyes, Grace. I'm going to remove the glasses, but I want to observe your eyes and the reaction to light from the get-go."

"They're closed, Doctor."

The weight on her face disappeared. "Okay, I'm going to stand to the side to observe your eyes. Make sure to tell me if anything has changed. Go ahead and open them."

After taking a deep breath, she opened her eyelids and squeaked, shutting them again.

Because instead of the usual blankness, or darkness as sighted people tended to say, there had been changes throughout.

"Did it hurt, Grace?"

"No, it surprised me. The usual solid nothingness changed."

"Do you think you can open your eyes and study straight in front of you? Maybe try to tell me what you see? I set something up on purpose, to judge how much detail is visible to you now."

Since her heart raced, some of her tiredness had temporarily faded. She could do this.

Slowly, she lifted her eyelids and blinked, focusing on the changes.

There was something that was almost the same size as her breast—at least from what she'd felt over the years. No, several somethings. They weren't on the floor, either, but on what must be a table. And everything was a bit fuzzy and slightly more solid than what had to be a wall behind it.

But how could she explain that to Dr. Vale? She didn't know what words to use. There was no way Grace would talk about her breast with him, no matter if he was a doctor.

Dr. Vale's voice broke the silence. "You can use your hands to help show me what's different. Over time, you'll learn visual descriptive words. But for now, just try to explain or show to the best of your ability what you see."

Using her hand, she made the round shape. "Many things like this, sitting on something that must be a table."

"Good. Those are oranges in a bowl."

"Oranges," she murmured.

The citrusy smell filled her mind, and she tried to pair the scent with the image.

It should be simple, and yet trying to rethink the meaning of words made her even more tired.

Dr. Vale spoke. "You're exhausted, I can see that.

Two more questions and we'll get you to your room, okay? First, are you in pain?"

"Not really. There's some throbbing in my head, of course. And I'm tired. But it doesn't hurt anywhere near as much as when I broke my arm as a child."

"Good. The throbbing will last a day or two and then should start fading. If not, you need to tell me. As for the last thing, I want you to look at my voice and tell me what you see."

Turning her head, she sucked in a breath. Even if it was only lighter and darker tints of her usual blankness, she made out what had to be a pair of eyes, nose, and mouth of another person.

She saw a face.

Her eyes heated with tears, and one slipped down her cheek, all while she smiled.

"See me, do you?"

His lips had moved as he talked.

She saw a person. Maybe not in a variety of colors—as her brother had tried to describe them to her over the years and it didn't match Dr. Vale's face—but she saw someone.

Tears trickled down her face as she let out a sob. Dr. Vale hugged her gently as she cried, feeling silly and yet unable to stop.

Grace had no idea how much time passed, but once she quieted, exhaustion weighed her down.

Dr. Vale finally spoke. "I think you see better up close than far away. However, we'll test that tomorrow. For now, we need to get you to your room. And I'm sorry, Grace, but you'll need to wear the glasses until tomorrow, too. I'll give you another pair that's merely tinted to use alongside these blackout ones, plus some instructions. But let's get you upstairs first."

After lifting her head, Grace took in the doctor's face one last time and murmured, "Can I try this with Everett tomorrow? And maybe to look in a mirror?"

"Of course. I'll be present to observe and make sure everything is still okay. We should probably establish your light tolerance as well. But for now, let's get you upstairs, Grace. You can sleep as long as you like, and ring the bellpull next to the bed if you need anything. Can you stand?"

"Aye, I think so."

And after he placed the special blackout glasses on her face, Grace struggled to her feet, swaying a bit.

Dr. Vale said, "Let me help you."

He gently placed a hand under her elbow and at her arm. It helped, although it was going to take all of her remaining strength to walk down the hall.

You can do it, Grace. If you stumble too much or faint, Everett will hear of it and be rather growly and overprotective for the next week.

And she didn't want that. Not when all she wanted was to see as much of the world as she could now.

So she embraced her inner wolf and did her best to walk with Dr. Vale's help out of the door and into the hallway. One step in front of another, making her think she could reach her room.

But then she stumbled, and someone else caught her.

William Khan, the fae witch Dark Lord of London, was being guided to the upstairs parlor when a door opened on the ground floor and Dr. River Vale escorted a female wearing strange glasses out of the room.

She was pale with dark brown hair, and even with the black glasses, he remembered her eyes were blue.

Eyes he'd never forgotten.

He'd met her before, after all. Grace Black was the younger sister of his fellow Dark Lord, Everett.

He watched as River struggled to lead her down the hall, but the female stumbled and teetered to one side. Without thinking, he rushed to her side and steadied the female with a hand under her arm.

She stilled and turned her head toward him.

Even though he couldn't see her eyes, he guessed they were probably widening. The blind often relied on scent to identify people, and he wondered if she remembered his.

From the one time he'd met her, when he'd been rude and brusque to her.

But William had no choice—he was that way with everyone. It was to protect them and save them from his powers. Because he'd lapsed once years ago, and it'd hurt someone he cared about.

And he would never allow that to happen again. Especially when so many people relied on him now.

Quickly releasing her, William backed several steps away as River Vale helped steady the shifter female. He cleared his throat and forced his voice to be his usual detached-yet-firm tonc. "I beg your pardon, Miss Black. I hope you are steady now." He glanced at Vale. "I'll wait upstairs."

Without another word, he turned and strode purposefully away from the female.

From the soft, warm female he wanted to help and protect, and to do so much more to. Ever since the first time he'd met her, he'd wanted to seek her out again.

But Grace Black wasn't for him.

No female was.

Before memories could rush forth, he focused on everything he needed to do today. Between the kidnapped fae witches and the possible enemies lurking in his territory—at least according to his latest report on the French vampires—he couldn't afford to be distracted.

By the time he reached the parlor, he was firmly in control and waited on the far side of the room, like he always did.

Like he always would.

Chapter Seven

Shopping in Victorian London had been quite the experience. Meadow was used to ordering things online, hoping they might fit, and sadly returning almost everything because it was too small or giant or simply unflattering.

But here? Nora had taken her to something called a modiste, who measured and made garments to order. Sure, they'd altered a few pre-made pieces so Meadow had something to wear after the modiste had tsked at her ruffled shirt and said that Meadow should never wear ruffles again. But after Nora put in a large order for her, Meadow exited the shop wearing a skirt and shirt that fit her. And while she would always yearn for soft pajamas, the modiste had provided some kind of loose corset that was more comfortable than any bra she'd ever worn before.

There was definitely something to having custom-made clothing.

Once they entered the main hall of her brother's place, the butler—a butler!—approached them and said to Nora, "Mrs. Vale, the Dark Lord is waiting for Miss Vale upstairs."

Meadow touched the bracelet around her wrist as her heart raced. From the bits and pieces she'd heard while shopping, she'd learned about William Khan's powers—he was the Wielder of Nightmares.

Meaning he could make anyone see their worst fears, and possibly even scare them to death.

Resisting a shiver, Meadow took a few deep breaths. He wouldn't do that to her; he just wouldn't. After all, Khan was interested in Yesenia's growing powers, and that should protect Meadow.

Maybe.

Nora touched her hand. "It's okay, Meadow. Khan is more than fair. He didn't have to allow a vampire to live in his territory, and yet he was the one to suggest I move here. He will be fair with you, too."

"How much does he know about me?"

"Oh, Leo already told him about Laurie and Joseph, and he knows you're from the future. But you should head upstairs and go talk with him. Especially since Khan hates to be kept waiting."

Nodding, Meadow went up the stairs, careful to lift her skirt so she wouldn't trip. The last thing she needed was to arrive with a bloody nose after falling on her face.

Although given her past luck, it wouldn't surprise her.

However, somehow Meadow made it up the stairs

without incident and stopped in front of the door to the parlor. She knocked, and a deep voice told her to enter.

After turning the knob, she opened the door and went inside. It took her a second to find Khan, who stood next to the fireplace on the opposite side of the room, leaning against the mantel.

He was tall and lean but not too thin, with broad shoulders. She couldn't make out his eyes, but thought they might be dark brown. His black hair was nearly to his shoulder—overly long for the current fashion she'd seen today—and his skin was a medium brown.

But what stood out to her was how he was positioned as far away as possible from the door or any of the chairs. Had he planned that on purpose?

Khan spoke up. "Please shut the door and sit down, Miss Vale. We have much to discuss."

Well, at least he wasn't calling her ma'am, like some teenagers at the grocery store had started to do. Twenty-six wasn't *that* old.

She sat, rearranged her skirts, and folded her hands in her lap. Her brother and Nora had advised her to wait and allow Khan to speak first. While the whole idea of a fae witch lord was still weird to her, she wasn't about to piss him off over something so minor. After all, this male would decide her fate in this time period.

He finally spoke again. "You're wearing a training bracelet. Does that mean you're not in control of your powers? And why? Did you not receive the necessary instruction?"

She nearly covered the bracelet on her wrist, but

resisted. "How much has Yesenia told you about our father?"

"That he wished to sell the use of you and your brother's powers to the highest bidder."

Yesenia must trust Khan at least a little to tell him that. "Yes. And not long after my powers manifested at eighteen, my father decided my powers could make him rich, uncaring that I didn't want to do what he planned. So Yesenia helped me escape into hiding. While she found a mentor of sorts for me, she wasn't a teacher. And so I learned what I could, but something must be wrong with me because I can't always control my magic. Not like River, or most fae witches, for that matter."

He studied her for a few seconds, probably wondering what he would do with a defective fae witch, before replying, "Has a tracker ever assessed you?"

A tracker was a fae witch who, after touching another fae witch once, could locate them anywhere using magical ley lines. They also could determine a person's powers, both main and secondary.

"Er, no. In my time, they're rare and used by various militaries to track threats and spies. Usually someone with a secondary tracking ability assesses our magic."

"So you don't know if you have any secondary powers then."

"No. Just the ability to control lust and desire."

She bit her tongue from saying it was a shitty power and she wished she could have anything else, even if it meant she could only control spiders.

And she hated spiders.

Meadow fidgeted, her fingers gripping her skirt and releasing it as Khan continued to stare. Did he ever blink?

He finally replied, “My most skilled tracker will meet with you tomorrow to determine all of your powers, and then I will send you a magic teacher. Not the same one as Yesenia, since Rebecca’s experience with time-wielders is too valuable. However, you are not the first person to control lust and desire, and if you become skilled in wielding it, then it could become lucrative for you. Many will want to hire you, such as the two vampires you blooded.”

She barely had time to digest the Dark Lord’s words about getting a magic teacher before he brought up Laurie and Joseph. “Excuse me? What? They want me to help in their sex club?”

Had Khan’s lips just twitched, or had she imagined it?

Considering his voice was the same cool, firm tone as earlier, she must have. He said, “They run a pleasure house, one that fae witches have been hesitant to use. However, it is popular with shifters, vampires, and humans. And yes, having a fae witch on hand to stir and amplify lust on demand will help their business, and maybe even encourage some of our kind to use it, if you’re there.”

With so much happening over the last day, she hadn’t thought of that. Of course Laurie and Joseph would try to woo her—she’d probably be able to increase their profits.

Khan's voice was a little more gentle when he said, "It may not be the only reason they wish to better know you, Meadow. However, it is something to keep in mind. Because the only way a fae witch can stay permanently in the vampire territory is to marry one, or in your case, two. Normally, I would give you two weeks to decide if that's what you want. However, since your training will take up a lot of your time in the coming weeks, I will give you a month to freely enter and leave the vampire territory without having to ask my permission. Although you will need to check in with either Yesenia or Reika Riley, who is a half-fae witch and married to a half-vampire named Stone. They can verify what you say and let me know if something seems strange, such as if you're being forced to do something against your will."

She sat up straighter. "I have boundaries and won't hesitate to tell Laurie or Joseph."

It was something she'd learned to do. Because when her powers leaked out, if she didn't stand strong, someone could've assaulted her.

Hence why she'd kept a baseball bat in her bedroom, for whenever her powers had leaked out.

Although they'd always stopped when she'd asked, come to think of it. Maybe she had a secondary power she didn't know about?

Khan raised an eyebrow. "Ah, but I didn't say it would be Laurence or Joseph that would make you do anything. Your powers are more powerful than you may realize, Meadow. Entire governments could be toppled if a male is convinced to sleep with the wrong person, especially since humans in this time are rather prudish, far more than we are. If your powers are strong enough, then paranormal-hating enemies wouldn't hesitate to kidnap you and use you for who knows what purposes."

"They would kidnap me? Really?"

Just how many dangers did she face in the late nineteenth century?

Khan replied, "I will have my tracker explain everything in more detail, along with your magic teacher. They will arrive tomorrow morning, and so your pass to leave the fae witch territory will start tomorrow afternoon, provided you follow any and all instructions from my tracker and your magic teacher." He stood up straight. "I think I have what I need for now."

As he made to leave, she blurted, "Will I get my own magic training bracelet? I had to borrow Yesenia's."

"Maybe. I don't think Yesenia will need it any longer, especially since you're here."

"But—"

"I must leave. Take it up with your sister."

With that, he walked along the outside of the room and left.

With a huge sigh, Meadow leaned back in the chair and crossed her arms over her chest. While part of her was excited to learn from an actual magic teacher and maybe get better control of her powers, part of her worried that maybe she was defective and no amount of training would help. After all, Stacey had been kind and done the best she could to instruct her. It wasn't as if her mentor had merely waved a hand and said to wing it.

There was a knock on the door, and Meadow stated, "Come in."

Nora appeared, with River right behind her. Meadow's brother looked grouchy, which didn't bode well.

Nora said, "Laurie and Joseph are here and have been waiting for Dark Lord Khan to leave. Would you like to see them? We can stay and offer support, if needed."

She eyed her older-yet-younger brother and at his stony eyes, she knew his being in the same room as Laurie and Joseph would be a bad idea. Besides, what could go wrong in a parlor, with her brother, sister-in-law, and who knew how many servants just a shout away?

And it would only fast-track the two vampires' eventual rejection of her, anyway. Oh, she'd let them claim her and bite her once. Hell, she could do with an orgasm or two. Even if they only wanted her because of fate, it'd been way too long since she'd dared to sleep with a guy.

Once the deed was done, they could go back to their lives, and she could go back to being alone, dealing with her powers.

Because no matter what Khan might believe, Meadow thought she might be broken.

"Meadow? Are you okay?" her brother asked.

She met River's gaze and forced a smile. "It's just a

lot, is all. But yes, I'll meet with Laurie and Joseph. Alone, though. Because as much as I love you, River, you can be overprotective and growly when it comes to family. And I don't want you to scare them off."

Nora snorted, but River replied, "It would take a hell of a lot more to scare them off than a few glares. Remember, I had to convince Laurie and Leo that I loved and wanted to marry Nora."

The pair shared a loving glance, and jealousy stabbed Meadow's heart.

Stop it. River deserves this. And even from what little you know about Nora, she deserves it, too.

River finally met Meadow's gaze again and nodded. "All right. But if I hear a single shout or loud noise, I'm fucking barging in here. They really should have more patience, the bastards, and give you a chance to settle in."

Meadow rolled her eyes. "Imagine being a vampire, River. And after decades of a still heart and the inability to eat or feel desire, you suddenly can. You'd probably be impatient too."

He grimaced. "I know with your powers it's unavoidable, but I'd rather not talk about desire with my little sister."

"So I'm still your little sister even though I'm older now?"

He strode across the room and put out a hand. Once she took it, he yanked her up and engulfed her in a hug. "Of course you're my little sister. You always will be."

The familiar warmth and scent of her brother

made her eyes heat with tears. "I know we tease and joke, or at least we used to. But I love you, River, and I'm glad we're together again."

He squeezed once more and released her. "Me too, Em. Me too."

Meadow noticed Nora wiping her eyes with a handkerchief. The vampire said, "Don't mind me. The baby makes me cry at everything."

River rushed to Nora's side and placed a hand over her belly. "Are you all right, love? Do I need to check on our little one again?"

"I'm fine, River." She wiped her face once more and then smiled at Meadow. "I'll ensure some tea and cakes are sent up. Unless you want something stronger?"

She shook her head. "If I'm only going to be claimed once by a pair of vampires, then I'd rather be sober and be able to remember it."

River frowned at her. "You're not doing that in here today, are you?"

"No. But if I drink too much, it might happen."

"Then no alcohol when your vampire pair is here." He studied her for a beat before asking, "Are you sure you want to do this today? I haven't even had the chance to ask about what Khan said to you."

"We can talk later, River. Putting off Laurie and Joseph will only make me more anxious, and I want to be as calm as possible when I start my magic lessons tomorrow with a real teacher."

"So Khan is giving you a magic teacher, then. I had a feeling he might."

Before she could reply, she heard someone coming up the stairs, along with low voices.

Male voices that had to belong to Laurie and Joseph.

Nora tugged River's arm. "Come on, darling. Let's leave them so they can get to know each other."

River murmured something Meadow couldn't hear, probably to the other males, and soon he and Nora were gone. Then Joseph appeared in the doorway, bowed his head, and entered. Laurie did the same little bowing of his head, and then shut the door.

But instead of coming closer, they merely stayed near the door. It was Joseph who spoke up. "You look lovely in your new clothes."

Meadow's cheeks heated, and she resisted the urge to straighten her skirts. "I look better, but skirts make me look like a whale."

Joseph frowned. "Not even a little."

She opened her mouth, but Laurie beat her to it. "You *are* beautiful, Meadow, and any male who says otherwise is mad." He took a few steps closer, stopping about a foot in front of her. He reached out a hand and lightly traced her cheek, her chin, and then down her neck, and she barely resisted shivering at his light touch. His voice was lower when he continued, "You wore your hair up to tease us, didn't you? To display all that soft skin, with your pulse beating faster and faster, to entice us."

He traced the side of her neck, no doubt over her artery, up and down. Each stroke sent a rush of heat through her.

How could such a light touch affect her so much? Not even kissing the last guy she'd tried to have sex with had turned her on like this.

Probably because her powers had leaked out in the past, and so there hadn't been any attempt at foreplay.

She gripped her bracelet, reassuring herself that it was still there.

Joseph walked closer and said, "No, it's not your magic, Meadow. Or even that you blooded us. I almost don't want to bring you to Nyx's Kingdom because too many males and females will try to win you away from us."

She frowned. "Stop being ridiculous." He was about to reply, but she spoke first and asked, "What's Nyx's Kingdom? Is that the name of your sex club?"

Laurie chuckled, all while still stroking her neck. "A pleasure house is what we call it. But yes, that's the name. Nyx is a lesser-known Greek goddess of night and darkness, which suits us. Not just because we're vampires, but also because a lot of people find the most pleasure during the night hours. Not all, but many."

Maybe if she were charming like her brother, she'd make a joke or innuendo. However, after being a near recluse for eight years, Meadow didn't have any practice. Instead, she blurted, "You don't have to try and woo me. I've already decided that I'll let you claim me, maybe even sooner rather than later. That way you can go back to your lives and let me figure out my own."

Laurie stilled his movements, and Joseph moved to

stand next to him. They both frowned at her, and she resisted twisting her hands in her lap.

Great. Had she just upset them? Or had they taken it as an invitation?

If so, fine. From her experience, after a bite and a few pumps, they'd be done and go to sleep, anyway. Then she'd never have to see them again.

Although a part of her wished it could be more than that.

But if there was one thing Meadow was not, it was optimistic.

So she merely steeled herself for what they said next, determined to make the best of the situation.

Chapter Eight

Joseph saw in Meadow some of the same fear he'd had in himself, back when he'd first met Laurie on the streets of London all those years ago.

After sharing a glance with Laurie—who nodded, acknowledging he'd let Joseph handle this first—he sat on the sofa opposite Meadow and leaned his elbows on his knees. Laurie moved over to the fireplace and merely watched.

Meadow glanced between them and played with her skirt. The urge to go over, place his hands over hers, and tell her she didn't need to fret around them was strong.

However, she'd known them less than two days, not to mention her life had just been thrown into chaos and completely changed without her consent. In time, he hoped she wouldn't feel anxious around them, but they weren't there yet.

So he kept his gaze on her face and asked, "How many years were you in hiding?"

She blinked, probably expecting him to say yes, they'd claim her now and get it over with.

But Joseph was patient, and he merely waited. Eventually she whispered, "Eight years."

"Which probably felt like twice that, right?"

"Er, yes. But what does that have to do with anything?"

He threaded his fingers together and replied, "Well, I understand a little about what you went through. You see, I spent five years on the streets, doing my best to survive after I saw my parents murdered when I was twelve."

Her eyes widened. "What?"

"It's true, but let's back up a bit so you can maybe understand me a little better. Is that okay?" She nodded, and Joseph pushed aside the urge to change the topic. If he didn't take this step, he didn't know if Meadow would ever give them a chance.

So even though he'd never told anyone but Laurie about his full past, Joseph took a deep breath and continued. "My parents came to this country not long before I was born. Before that, they had been fighting to end the slave trade of humans and paranormals as part of the largest resistance army in Northern Africa. When it came time to send representatives to the United Kingdom to try persuading the humans to change their laws, my parents were selected; they even changed their last name to Hope in an effort to show their dedication. And while it took them nearly thirteen years to do it, they succeeded in helping to get the Slavery Abolition Act passed in Parliament.

"However, once the law abolishing slavery in the British Empire passed in 1833, there were a lot of people who blamed my parents for destroying their businesses. And despite their every precaution, a group of humans finally found them and killed them. However, right before the mob of people broke into our house, my parents hid me in a secret compartment in the wall. And through the cracks in the boards, I saw everything, only keeping quiet because I'd promised my mother I'd do so."

Meadow placed a hand over her mouth. "Oh, Joseph, I'm so sorry."

Even decades later, he remembered his parents standing up to the mob despite knowing they had no chance.

And him trying not to scream or cry because he'd always kept his promises to his mother; he'd wanted her to be proud until the end.

Before more awful memories of that day could rush back, he took a deep breath and pressed on. The sooner he got all of this out, the better. "Thank you. As you can imagine, it broke me a little. I wanted to stay and organize their funerals, but whilst watching my parents being murdered, the ringleader had put a bounty on my head. So once it was dark, I slipped out the back and ran.

"After that, I spent the next five years living in the shadows, struggling to stay warm or even eat, but determined to live and find my parents' killers. And I might've stayed that way forever, full of anger and distrust, if not for Laurie."

Joseph looked at Laurie, and the vampire male smiled, probably remembering how Joseph had saved him from a group of street boys.

Focusing back on Meadow, he continued, "My point is that I've had decades to come to terms with what happened and to accept that I don't have to stay in the shadows any longer. Even my parents' killers were brought to justice and hanged. However, you have just come out of hiding. And whilst you didn't watch anyone get murdered, you were always watching over your shoulder for danger and keeping people at arm's length to protect them. I have no doubt it took its toll, didn't it?"

He barely heard her reply. "Yes."

The sadness in her voice shot straight to his heart. Right then and there, Joseph decided he wanted to bring some light and joy into her life, even if she didn't want them forever.

Although he was going to try his bloody best to ensure her future was with them.

Focus. This is the first step in helping Meadow deal with her pain. "You don't have to isolate yourself like that any longer, Meadow." She frowned and opened her mouth, but he beat her to it. "I know you're going to say something about platitudes, and how we want to fuck and bite you to complete the claiming, and then walk away. But we want more than that, if you'll give us a chance."

"Why, though? I don't understand why you want me so badly?"

Joseph secretly wished he could punish the males in her time who'd made her feel so unwanted.

However, they weren't here; Meadow was. So he said, "Because I see a soul who wants to be loved and cherished and accepted. And those are all things we want to give you, to desperately help you fill the holes in your heart as you do the same for us. That might be a bit too much honesty this early, but I'm always honest. All we're asking for is a chance. One where you don't dismiss us or think we want to fuck you and leave."

She searched his gaze for a few seconds and then did the same for Laurie. Finally she replied, "I heard you two were together before, and you must be over the moon to be able to have sex with each other again. You don't need me."

Ah, well, their fae witch was just as blunt as her siblings. Not that he minded. It should make things easier.

He motioned for Laurie to come over, and he sat next to Joseph before looking at Meadow. "Whilst it's true Joseph and I were together before, we've only ever truly been happy when there was also a female for us to take care of, and treasure, and love. We both have so much to give, the need to care for, and maybe it's difficult for others to understand, but it makes sense to us. Although yes, we love each other, and any female who joins us will have to accept that, along with our love for her too. Is that a problem for you?"

"Er, no. I've met a lot of poly-pairings over the years, in my line of work. Sometimes, it just works for people, while others only ever want a single lover."

Laurie asked, "And yourself? If you had the perfect future, what would it look like?"

She glanced between them and then bit her bottom lip. It took everything Joseph had not to imagine taking her soft lip between his teeth as he waited for her reply.

LAURIE HADN'T EXPECTED to ask Meadow what she wanted so soon. And yet, in a way, he was glad. Given how easily he usually lost his heart, it was better to know now.

Even if she didn't want them.

Although after hearing about how she'd been in hiding so long, probably self-isolating more than normal because of her magic, Laurie wanted more than ever for her to give him and Joseph a chance. She was damaged, more so than even Joseph had been when Laurie had first met him, and he wanted to show her affection and caring and to make her laugh.

And drive her wild with his mouth before letting her come. And to let her know it was all because he wanted to give her pleasure, and not because of her powers.

Because it'd been a long time since he'd met someone who had such a low opinion of their attraction and beauty. Her hazel eyes were a mixture of brown and green, with even a few flecks of blue. And with her hair pulled away from her face, showing off her long neck, he wanted to nuzzle and kiss and nibble until she begged for more.

But more than that, Laurie wanted to watch her walk through Nyx's Kingdom with her head held high like a queen, with some patrons thanking her for helping them to overcome their hesitations and shame.

Because yes, their pleasure house was about sex and orgasms and fun, but they also liked to help their patrons embrace their true desires and selves.

However, he was getting ahead of himself. He focused on Meadow, wanting to hear her answer.

She placed her hand over her training bracelet and tapped it before she replied, "I-I'm not against a threesome. Although I've never tried it, to be fair. My sexual experiences have been, well, crappy. But there is one thing I need to know—will you focus on your own orgasms or will you think of mine, too? Because if you're like the other males from my past, who think only of themselves, then I don't want that or you beyond the claiming."

Laurie frowned. "Who the bloody hell never ensured your pleasure as well?"

She blinked. "Er, all of them. Granted, it's been, what, three males? But still, they basically thrust a few times, groaned, and rolled over. While I usually unleashed my powers with my back turned or in a separate room for my old job, I know there should be more. But it's probably only that way when magic is involved, isn't it?"

He shared a glance with Joseph, both of them

better understanding Meadow's hesitation and poor view of sex.

Joseph spoke up. "We rarely have a fae witch use her magic at our pleasure house, and usually only for certain requests, such as ice or pain play. And most couples or groups enjoy themselves, male or female. I can't speak for everyone, but for us, ensuring another's orgasm is like a challenge, and making them come is the reward. I would offer to show you now what I can do with just my fingers, but I won't. It'll probably be better for you to visit the pleasure house and see others, and then you'll know we aren't lying just to claim you. The voyeur rooms might be a good place to start, as they want others to watch. And you can wear your training bracelet the whole time."

"Um, you want me to watch people having sex?"

Laurie smiled. "Only if you truly want to. But if you want proof that multiple partners can and will try to please each other, one of our regular foursomes will be using the room tomorrow night. Would you like to see? Either from behind a wall with a viewing slit, or even from one of the chairs in the room, it'll be up to you."

"With you two?"

"You can go alone, if you wish."

He almost hoped she did, then maybe she'd allow them to help her release some tension afterward.

But no matter what, Laurie was determined to show her it could be good, even without magic. And if she allowed them to show her, then he and Joseph would make sure that it was something she'd never forget.

MEADOW'S HEART thudded as she imagined watching others have sex and enjoy it, all without magic, and her core throbbed.

Sure, she'd known in books that males always ensured their females orgasmed too, maybe a few times, before thrusting into her. However, those were books and not reality, and Meadow thought maybe they were just comfort reads for disappointed females.

Although, as she looked between Laurie and Joseph and noted the heat in their gazes, she wondered if her self-isolation and fear of her powers had skewed her views. Maybe males caring about their females was more common in real life than she'd previously thought. After all, her experience boiled down to her stirring desire for others, or sleeping with young twenty-somethings she'd barely known.

And even though she'd facilitated desire and lust and had used her powers to do so—and was more than used to the sounds and smells that went along with it—she hesitated. Because this would be for her, merely out of curiosity, and afterward she'd have to meet again with Laurie and Joseph, and she might get bold and ask for a demonstration.

Which she shouldn't do. Despite their talk about both of them wanting her, and that she was beautiful, and all that, she still thought she would get in the way.

After all, they'd known each other for decades. Why would they want an intruder in their midst?

Especially someone as boring and fluffy as her?

"Meadow," Laurie said. Once she met his gaze again, he continued, "You can think about it and decide later. We're not here to pressure you. But did Khan give you permission to visit the vampire territory?"

She jumped at the change of subject. "Yes, from tomorrow evening, that is. I need to meet with his tracker and my magic teacher first."

"Perfect." He reached into his coat, took out a black card with gold paint, and held it out to her. "This will allow you to enter Nyx's Kingdom. Mention your name, and our top steward will escort you wherever you wish."

"Not you two?"

Laurie replied, "If you want us to accompany you, then mention it to Oliver Jones. He'll find us. But one more thing about that card—until the claiming is complete, it won't allow you to partner anyone else inside."

Meadow frowned. "Wait, you'd allow me to jump into the arms of another right after?"

"I hope not, and I have faith we'll convince you otherwise. But that's in the future, and we're not here to dictate what you must do. However, until you allow us to claim you, our vampire's instinct for you will intensify. And to avoid causing a fight, or worse, please don't invite anyone else into your bed, male or female. Will you promise?"

She stared at the card. There was a design of a woman in a flowing gown, and something written in the old vampire language that people only studied in universities back in her time.

But no matter what it said, the thick paper and gold paint felt so much heavier than they were.

Even so, Laurie and Joseph were giving her space and the chance to see what she'd never experienced herself, at least without magic. And it wasn't as if she were going to have people lining up to bed her, or anything.

So she nodded, replied, "I promise."

Laurie asked, "Will you come tomorrow? We can even provide a demi-mask, if you want to be anonymous."

She finally met his eyes again. They were deep brown with flecks of amber, and a little inset. However, combined with his straight nose and soft-in-a-masculine-way lips, he was quite attractive. Willing her cheeks not to flush, she said, "Yes, I'd like one."

Joseph spoke up. "We'll send you an outfit as well. Our modiste has collaborated with the one you visited today, so she'll get your measurements."

Her gaze moved to Joseph. His eyes were more serious, but the dark brown drew her in, almost inviting her to learn more about him. Maybe as his lips kissed down her neck.

Stop it, Meadow. All this talk of sex clubs was getting to her.

She answered, "If it's even possible to get something made so quickly. Just don't put me in a teddy with a feather boa." At their confused looks, she clarified, "Nothing too revealing. I won't feel comfortable walking around in my underwear."

Laurie and Joseph shared a glance—they did that a lot and seemed to have entire conversations without speaking, which made her a little jealous—and Joseph finally replied, "Of course not. We would never embarrass you or force you to wear something that made you uncomfortable."

In other words, they wouldn't want everyone watching her rolls wobble.

Meadow's desire instantly died. Maybe going to the sex club was a bad idea.

As she tried to think of a polite way to decline, Joseph's hand covered hers. She should move her own hands away. But as his thumb stroked her skin, some of her anxiety faded.

"Look at me, Meadow."

She did, right into Joseph's gorgeous eyes. Ones with longer eyelashes than any male should have.

As he continued to stroke the back of her hand, he stated, "You are beautiful, Meadow Vale." His free hand cupped her cheek, and against her better judgement, she leaned into his touch. "Who convinced you otherwise?"

Closing her eyes, she tried to block out first her father's words and then those of the males she'd slept with, but two slipped through.

After her father knocked a bowl out of her hands, he shouted, "You don't need to eat anything else. How can I use you and your powers to seduce powerful people if you're too fat for anyone to want to fuck?"

Her first supposed boyfriend, after he took her virginity, had rolled out of bed a few minutes afterward and dressed as he said, "I expected your magic to make that better. It's probably the only reason I got hard at all. Don't call me again. Without your magic, who would ever get aroused with such a fucking ugly female?"

It was only when someone brushed tears from her cheek that she realized she was crying. Forcing her eyes open, she saw both Laurie and Joseph in front of her, them both wiping her tears away.

Laurie whispered, "Meadow, what's wrong?"

Joseph added, "It will stay with us, and no one else, we promise."

As she glanced between them, she wanted to tell them. Oh, how she wanted to finally unburden the horrible memories. She'd barely ever seen her siblings after going into hiding, and when she had, she hadn't wanted to ruin the precious stolen moments by sharing her troubles.

But these males were strangers. Why would they care?

And yet, something about them made her want to try.

However, her tears turned into sobs. And before she knew it, she was being carried to the sofa, soon sitting in Laurie's lap while leaning against Joseph's shoulder, crying and crying, unable to stop.

Chapter Nine

Joseph stroked Meadow's back while Laurie stroked her hair and cheek, and he burned to know who or what had made her cry. It was something in her past, no doubt. Some person or more had made her feel unworthy or lesser, and he didn't like it.

However, in this moment, Meadow merely needed to let out her emotions. She'd kept them bottled up, probably for years, and if all he and Laurie could do right now was hold and comfort her, then it was enough.

Eventually her sobs quieted, and she leaned more heavily against Joseph's chest. Laurie stroked her hair back from her face before pressing his cheek to hers. Joseph tightened his arm around Meadow's waist, and they both remained quiet while also letting her know they were there for her.

After another minute or two, she whispered, "I'm sorry."

"Why?" Joseph asked.

She avoided looking at either of them. "For crying all over you. That's probably not what you expected from the female who blooded you."

Laurie wrapped his arm over Joseph's and around Meadow until she was being held closely between them. He asked, "Do you feel a little better now?"

"Er, I guess so."

"Then that makes me happy. How about you, Joseph?"

Joseph lifted his free hand and gently took Meadow's chin between his fingers. Her eyes finally met his, and he hated the embarrassment there. Taking a chance, he kissed her forehead. When she didn't tense or pull away, he did it again before leaning back and saying, "We always want you to be honest with us. I'm sure you'll call us out on things, and we might not like it and get grumpy, but everyone needs others to hold them accountable sometimes. Especially with three people, communication will be important."

She glanced at Laurie and then back at Joseph. "Since when do males want to talk and be open? They've never liked it before, in my experience."

He grunted. "Then they were probably insecure arseholes who wanted someone in their bed and not a true partner."

She glanced down again. "Maybe."

There was more to that single word, but Joseph didn't want to push too far too fast. So he focused back on his point. "And when it comes to honesty, we want you to feel comfortable being yourself. We all have good, bad, and ugly pieces, and sharing them can help you become more comfortable with yourself, others, and the world. I know it did for me."

Laurie nuzzled his cheek against Meadow's. "It's true, but also bloody difficult to do when you're not used to it. It took me years to get Joseph to talk with me, to convince him I wouldn't betray his trust."

"You know why, Laurie. I thought for years that someone was looking to kill me."

"I know, but didn't you feel better once you told me more?"

He grunted. "Maybe."

Laurie grinned, and Joseph saw Meadow's lips twitch from the corner of his eye.

Much better, he thought.

Laurie looked back at Meadow and said, "We mean it, though, that you can tell us anything and we won't share your secrets. Ever." He smiled at her. "So if you ever want to share why you cried just now, we'll listen. It might help, whenever you're ready to do it."

One of Meadow's hands played with the back of Laurie's hand, and the other traced shapes on Joseph's chest. Her gaze remained fixed to the side, and she looked lost in thought.

Would she share? He wanted to shout about how she should. After all, sharing with Laurie not long after they'd met had eased something inside him. He'd been embarrassed to cry a little at seventeen, but he'd kept it bottled up so long that it'd been necessary. Thankfully, Laurie hadn't judged him.

As Meadow fought some internal battle, Joseph

merely reveled in holding her, with Laurie next to him, realizing how much he'd missed this. Having a third person with them, sharing such an important moment, and how he and Laurie banded together to make her feel safe and wanted and to be what she needed.

Eventually Meadow's voice brought him back to the present. "I'm sure you guys have things to do, though. More important things than listening to me."

Laurie replied, "We don't have anything important until tomorrow afternoon. Until then, we're here for you."

She continued to play with Joseph's tie for a few more seconds before saying, "Has my sister shared much about our father?"

Joseph frowned. "Yesenia? A little, but not much. Just enough to let everyone know you could be in danger, and that's why she was so focused on bringing you to the past."

Her voice was low, but vampires had supersensitive hearing, so they heard everything.

"My father wanted to be a super successful con artist, or snake oil salesman, or what might you call it here? Someone who uses charm and lies to get money and other things that they want?"

"Charlatan, maybe?" Laurie said.

"That sounds about right. At any rate, he married both my mother and Yesenia's mother because of their family's wealth and connections. Both died young, and when I was older, I heard the rumors about how he'd constantly abused and harassed and belittled them. My mother burned out on her magic because my father kept pushing her so he didn't have to work, and eventually she jumped off a building and killed herself."

Joseph and Laurie both tightened their hold on Meadow. The thought of her mother's husband using her to the point she burned out—which was a serious condition for a fae witch—made Joseph want to do some harm. Laurie's gaze said the same thing.

And Meadow hadn't even gotten to the part that involved herself.

Calm down, Joseph. She needs support, and anger won't help anything right now.

He took a deep breath and managed to focus solely on Meadow when she spoke again. "When my mother died, my father tried to marry again. However, my grandparents and extended family, ones that I'd never met, ensured that the rest of the American fae witch community knew about him and what he did to his wives. And since he couldn't remarry to finance his laziness, he took risks and gambled and invested, and got into mountains of debt. Once Yesenia was deemed defective because they thought she didn't have any magic, he became obsessed with River and me. Once we reached adulthood and discovered our own magical abilities, he plotted every way he could make money off them. Mine, in particular, he wanted to use for power and money and control. Not just with my magic, but he also wanted to turn me into some sort of master seductress, one who could entice anyone and then subtly control them with my powers."

In other words, Meadow's father had wanted to use her as a fancy prostitute.

Just the thought of any daughter or son of his being made to do that, let alone by his direction, made Joseph want to hit something.

Laurie must've sensed his tension because he asked Meadow, "What else did he do? Because he's the reason you cried, isn't he? Either his actions, words, or both."

She bobbed her head. "It was mostly because of him. My first sort-of boyfriend was a jerk, but at least he wasn't my father. You know, the guy who was supposed to love and protect me? No, all he wanted was to turn me into a model-slash-secret-agent who could entice anyone by crooking my finger. He kept half-starving me, and when I got so hungry I tried to sneak something to eat, he sometimes found me and yelled at me for being a selfish, fat female who wanted to see her father homeless on the streets. Unless I was thin, I was of no use to him." Her voice lowered. "And when you're eighteen years old, with new magical powers that you're still trying to figure out, it's particularly devastating. Yesenia lived on her own by that point—our father had kicked her out—but when we met up in secret once, I nearly fainted and she heard a little about it. Within a month, she found me an unofficial mentor, and I went into hiding."

The more she revealed, the angrier Joseph got. How could her father do such a thing to his child? Joseph had experienced starvation on the streets a few times when young, especially when he hadn't had blood for weeks, and her father had forced her to endure it on purpose?

Meadow glanced at him and flinched. Before Joseph could calm himself enough to reply, Laurie did. "He's not mad at you, Meadow. Joseph rarely gets so angry he can't talk and looks thunderous, but if he feels even a fraction of the hatred and disdain I have for your father, then that's why he looks so upset."

Not trusting his temper yet, he merely nodded.

Laurie stroked Meadow's cheek to get her attention before saying, "Your father, if you can even call him that, is the reason you don't believe us when we say you're beautiful, isn't he?"

Meadow glanced away, the action confirming it.

Joseph met Laurie's eyes, and even though the other male seemed calm on the surface, Joseph could see his inner rage. It was up to them to convince Meadow that her father had been a lying, selfish bastard.

And if she came to Nyx's Kingdom tomorrow night, they'd start there.

BETWEEN CRYING and reliving memories of her father, Meadow struggled to stay awake. Especially sitting between Laurie and Joseph, who radiated heat and a sense of safety. It was strange, considering she barely knew them. And yet, they hadn't made fun of her, or dropped comments about how her father had been right, or dismissed her for being too emotional.

No, they were angry on her behalf. Nearly as much as Yesenia had been when Meadow had nearly fainted.

She still didn't understand why, though. Yes, she had blooded them both. But they couldn't seriously wish to have her permanently in their lives. Could they?

Before she could think too much about it and drain her remaining energy, Joseph kissed her forehead again. The warmth of his lips made her belly flip, and she almost asked him to kiss her on the mouth.

But he spoke before she could make that mistake. "You look as if you're about to fall asleep, Meadow. We'll carry you to your room and put you to bed."

For a half-second, she thought they'd join her.

However, Laurie added, "To sleep. We can either come back tomorrow, or you can come to Nyx's Kingdom. Just know that we're not running away or giving up. Far from it. You're just exhausted, pet, and need to get some sleep, is all."

If she were more outgoing, or bolder, or more confident, she'd ask them to stay.

She wasn't, though, and merely murmured, "I'll go to Nyx's Kingdom tomorrow."

Laurie nuzzled her cheek, and she nearly sighed. The slight bristle of his late-day stubble felt good.

Although was it late for them? Vampires always had weird schedules.

Maybe she should ask.

Then she yawned and struggled to keep her eyes open. She should probably say goodbye soon, or she might ramble and say things she regretted later.

"Bed, please, and we can meet again tomorrow."

Joseph took her into his lap. Laurie stood, and then scooped her into his arms. She tried to protest, but he merely held her closer and murmured, "You wouldn't make it up the stairs right now. Now, hush, and let me help you."

Exhausted, she merely nodded, wrapped her arms around his neck, and laid her head on his shoulder. Even though Laurie was a little shorter and leaner than Joseph, she felt his hard muscles against her side. She wondered if he'd frozen that way or if he'd gotten into shape later. Was that possible?

She really needed to get more information from Yesenia because Meadow didn't remember enough from her vampire studies.

Laurie's gait lulled her, and she kept closing her eyes and opening them, determined to be awake when they said goodbye and left.

Eventually, he placed her on a bed—the blanket folded down—and then tucked her in. He brushed the hair from her face and said, "Sweet dreams, beautiful. We're both looking forward to tomorrow."

Then Laurie was gone, and Joseph leaned over her. His jaw still looked tense, but he lowered his head and gently kissed her cheek, lingering for a few seconds. A deep longing crashed over her, to have both of them stay and keep her warm.

However, they were gone far too soon, and Meadow finally embraced her exhaustion and dreamed of all the ways visiting Nyx's Kingdom could go wrong.

Chapter Ten

The next day, Meadow paced in front of the fireplace, both eager and afraid to meet the tracker and her new magic teacher.

She'd received a note saying they'd come at two o'clock, and it was five past. There were probably traffic jams in this time, even if it was with horses and carriages instead of cars, but they had to come, didn't they? There was no way any fae witch in London would dare defy Dark Lord Khan.

But it was more than them being a few minutes late, of course, that made her anxious. She would leave for Laurie and Joseph's pleasure house later in the day, around 8 p.m. Her sister-in-law had suggested waiting until it was dark out since that's when more patrons would be milling about.

Even if she wasn't much of a night person, it made sense. And once Joseph had written back, saying the foursome would start at nine that evening in the voyeur room, she'd become more and more eager to go. She'd probably only peek through a slit in a wall to avoid anyone looking at her with disgust, because she wasn't sure she could handle that. At least, not when everything was so new and she was constantly afraid of getting things wrong.

Laurie's words from the night before rushed back to her: *Sweet dreams, beautiful. We both hope to see you tomorrow.*

Add in Joseph's lingering goodnight kiss, and it'd been like something out of a movie. Two guys who wanted her, and each other, and were more supportive in a matter of hours than any guy she'd tried to date before. In other words, they had to be too good to be true, right?

A knock made her jump, and Meadow placed a hand over her heart. *Focus, Meadow. Your future in the past relies on these people.*

Not to mention if her lessons went well, she might fully control her powers one day.

If that were possible, of course.

"Enter," she stated as she stood near one of the chairs.

A tall, pale female with red hair braided around her head, showing off her pointed ears, walked in, closely followed by another shorter female with long black hair and light brown skin.

The redhead smiled. "I'm Helena Watts, the tracker. And this is Nadia Ahmed, your new magic teacher."

Meadow eyed Nadia, who couldn't be more than

thirty, and before she could think better of it, she blurted, "Do you have the same powers as me?"

Nadia smiled at her. "I don't know if our secondary powers will match, if you have one. But yes, I also control lust and desire." She held up her hands to show off her wrists. "And soon enough, you'll be like me, and not have to wear anything to contain your magic."

"What's your secondary power?"

"Truth seeker."

Meadow blinked. Nadia could tell when someone was lying, no matter if they were a paranormal or human.

Nadia continued, "Which, to be honest, will probably help the both of us. I only use it when absolutely necessary, and since it's only my secondary power, it's not strong enough to coerce you to tell the truth. Anything you say will be of your own free will, and at your own pace. Although I hope you won't hold back too much. I'll admit, I'm interested in chatting with someone from the future. Not that you can tell me everything, of course."

The more Nadia talked, the less anxious Meadow became. She was almost…normal. It was as if she were chatting with her old mentor, Stacey.

Before sadness engulfed Meadow at memories of the only person she regretted leaving in the future, Helena walked over, garnering her attention. "We have a lot to discuss, of course. I think everything might go faster if you'll take my hand straight away."

She put out her hand, palm up, and waited.

Since Helena was a tracker, it meant as soon as

Meadow touched her, she would know all of her powers and discover her distinct magical signature, which all fae witches—even part ones—had.

However, over breakfast Yesenia—her sister had come to visit—had told her to trust Khan, and if nothing else, Meadow trusted her sister. So she gingerly placed her hand in Helena's.

A tingling warmth rushed up her arm and throughout her body before retreating. Once gone, Helena released her and quirked an eyebrow. "Do you wish to know your secondary power?"

"I have one?"

She nodded. "Yes. It's the power of persuasion, and when you think about it, when combined with lust and desire, that makes you fairly powerful. Although I trust you're not going to use it for selfish purposes?"

"Never. I ran away rather than allow my father to force me to use it for dishonest purposes."

"Good. Right, well, I'll ring the bell for tea and we can sit and chat. There's a lot to go over before we leave today."

Meadow was growing used to how everyone was obsessed with drinking tea and eating cakes with visitors. Although if someone had a lot of friends, then they'd probably be jittery from all the caffeine and sugar by the end of the day.

As she imagined some fae witch or vampire pacing and rambling about anything and everything from drinking too much tea, while guests tried to sit and look straight-faced, she nearly burst out laughing.

If Helena noticed Meadow's mirth, she didn't say.

Although Nadia walked closer and whispered, "My parents had to get used to it, too. They came here from Egypt, and tea is just a common drink there, drunk all day long, and the thought of it being special was strange to them. But I have to admit I enjoy the English-style pastries."

"Egypt? Wow. That had to be a big change, weather-wise."

She nearly asked if she'd seen the Pyramids of Giza or any of the other ancient Egyptian monuments, but then wondered if they were even visible in this time period. History had never been Meadow's strongest subject, and she was too embarrassed to ask.

Maybe her sister could recommend some books to help her figure out what did or didn't exist in 1890.

Nadia motioned for Meadow to sit, and then followed suit in a chair across from her before replying, "Things were difficult for them after yet another war with the Ottoman Empire, and so my parents took a chance on coming to the UK." She shrugged. "And it worked out, for the most part. Especially once Dark Lord Khan was finally able to establish peace here, as well as make a treaty with the Egyptian fae witches. So now my parents can sometimes visit their friends and family, which they couldn't do for many years."

"Dark Lord Khan really established peace with the Egyptian fae witches?"

"Oh, yes. Not to mention the vampires and shifters in the UK, too. He rarely speaks and seems aloof, but he knows how to persuade others to cooperate."

"So he has the power of persuasion too? I thought he was the Wielder of Nightmares?"

Helena had returned and sat down before jumping in. "He is, and that's the only power he confirms with the public. But it's one of the most powerful types of magic, as you can imagine, and is all he needs. He never threatens, but rumors are enough for others to be wary around him."

Meadow glanced between the two females, wondering if she should keep asking questions.

However, a maid came in with the tea tray, and Meadow held her tongue.

Once everyone had some tea and cookies, Helena looked at her and said, "Ask us whatever you wish, Meadow. We may not be able to answer everything, but we'll explain whatever isn't confidential."

After nibbling on a cookie, she replied, "We don't have lords back in my time, so I have no idea what to expect. If I misbehave or make a mistake, does that mean he'll unleash his powers on me?"

Helena shook her head. "Of course not. Nadia will not only help you with your magic but also with adjusting to this time period's rules, laws, and expectations. Dark Lord Khan has high standards, but is fair. If someone steps out of line, then there are various reprimands and punishments, depending on the offense. From what I've learned from Yesenia and River, it's similar to the American Fae Witch Council you have back home, albeit a little harsher. Khan hopes to eventually tear down the wall separating the paranormals living in the East End from the rest of

London, but knows he can't do it until he roots out rogue magic users and law-breakers."

In other words, fae witches who'd use their magic for money or power or retribution, much like her father had wanted to force his children to do.

Knowing Khan didn't tolerate that kind of stuff both made her a little more at ease, but also nervous. "What if I make a mistake before I'm fully trained? Or, what if I can't be fully trained?"

Nadia put her empty teacup down and patted Meadow's hand. "Don't get ahead of yourself. All I know is that you had a sort-of mentor, but no formal training. Is that correct?"

"Yes. I, well, I..." She hesitated, but after the two females merely waited patiently, she finally had enough nerve to add, "I had to run away about six months after my powers manifested because my father wanted to sell my magic to the highest bidder, and I stayed in hiding for about eight years. So, no, I didn't have any formal training. Stacey, my mentor, taught me as much as she could, but she'd never been a teacher before and claimed my magic was a lot stronger than hers."

Which was why she hadn't been able to teach Meadow how to control it well, unfortunately.

Nadia nodded. "Right, well, we'll start your formal lessons tomorrow. And I promise to be honest with you about how fast or slow we can do things, as long as you're honest with me, too."

"What about my secondary ability? Will you help me with that too?"

"Yes. If I have trouble, then Helena will help us. Her secondary power is persuasion as well."

As she glanced between the two females, who seemed confident they could help her, hope bloomed in her chest and Meadow's eyes heated. "Thank you."

"No worries," Nadia said. "As much as I'm excited to be your teacher, it also benefits every fae witch to have a trained population. We don't want to give the humans anything to use against us."

The latter sentence sounded bitter, but before Meadow could ask for details, Helena spoke up. "Not all humans are looking for an excuse to attack or kidnap or report us to the paranormal overseers, though. Rest assured, any that are inside your vampires' pleasure house will have been vetted thoroughly."

"They're not my vampires," Meadow murmured.

Helena smiled. "If you say so. Although I wish I'd blooded that pair. Handsome, rich, and with hearts of gold? That's a rare combination to find in one male, let alone two."

"What do you mean by hearts of gold?"

Helena shrugged. "They've done a lot to improve living conditions inside the vampire territory, and they also often help Laurie's nephew with rescue missions." She paused, studied Meadow for a few beats, and asked, "How much do you know of Nora's past?"

"Not a lot, just that it was bad. Like, really bad."

"It's not my story to tell, but her son, Ambrose, helps get males and females out of abusive situations, or worse. Nora runs safe havens for females who've escaped abusive families, partners, or sexual slavery, and Laurie and Joseph help fund those places. They even hire those willing to work in their business, or just their household section."

So Laurie and Joseph were not only sexy and caring, but rich and gave to charity?

She rubbed her forehead. They could have anyone, so why had fate given such great catches to her?

Nadia spoke again. "I can sense we're overwhelming you, and you may need a break soon. However, I need to let you know I left a small trunk with the butler and it should be in your room by now. There are some books and notes to help when you're ready to learn some more, as well as some blank journals. I want you to write in a journal each day, and make sure to include your feelings and frustrations. I'm the only other person who will see it, and since I'm a truth seeker, I'll be able to tell if you're lying, even with your writing. So, please, don't try to make things appear better than they are. I can't help you if I don't know what you're worrying about, or if you're struggling more than you show to the world."

The thought of someone reading about her worries and faults and troubles made her palms sweat. And yet, if she ever wanted a chance to be like other fae witches and not be afraid of her magic, she needed Nadia's help. "I'll try my best, although I've never kept a journal before. I was always too afraid someone would find it and alert my father to my location."

Especially once she'd lost contact with Yesenia and

River. She might know now that they'd been here in the past, but back then, she'd had no idea.

Nadia replied, "Trying is all I ask for. Unless you have any other pressing questions, I know Helena has a full schedule and you probably want to rest a little before visiting the vampire territory tonight."

Meadow shook her head. "I'm sure I'll have tons of questions later, but right now? My head is spinning and I don't even know where to start. Maybe writing out my thoughts will help me figure out what to ask tomorrow."

"That sounds fine. Bring your journal tomorrow, and we'll go from there."

Helena finished off her little cake before standing, and Nadia did the same. Meadow hurried to her feet too before Helena said, "If there is ever an emergency, and you're not with your siblings or Nadia, then go to the address on this card."

She handed over a white card, with an address scribbled in a barely legible hand. Well, apart from the first line, which said, "Fae Witch Council Building."

Helena gestured toward the card. "Any fae witch in the East End will know where that building is, and I'd recommend someone showing you where it is, too. Those who work inside the council building are trustworthy and won't try to steal from or assault you. Given what Yesenia has told me, your time is a lot safer, especially for females. And whilst most of the time this part of London is safe, there are still some criminals, like in any big city. But if anyone, I mean anyone, has a French accent, immediately return to one of your siblings' homes or to the Fae Witch Council building."

"Wait, so all French people, or paranormals, are being treated as enemies?"

Nadia pressed her lips into a firm line before saying, "I wish it didn't have to be that way, but too many fae witches have gone missing in recent months. And from what information we've learned, bystanders all heard French accents, and most of the kidnappers were vampires. It might be a ruse, it might not. But given our magical powers, Meadow, we especially need to be careful because it could become a powerful tool for an enemy."

Whatever peace she'd found chatting with the two females evaporated. "So I'll have to hide here too?"

Nadia shook her head. "No. As long as we're sensible and don't take risks, we'll be fine. My husband or brother-in-law is always with me after dark, and I can't leave the country any time soon. But it's better than becoming a prisoner of war."

"Wait, the British fae witches are at war?"

Helena replied, "Not yet, but I expect it'll happen soon. After the French vampires kidnapped Dark Lord Leopold's nephew and tortured him, they all but declared war since we're allies with the vampires and shifters in the UK. Only because the Dark Lords are trying to handle the situation more subtly have they not formally done so. If things become dire, you'll hear of it from your siblings or your brother-in-law."

It suddenly made sense why her brother had been so protective of Nora, and how he or a few armed footmen or guards had always accompanied her when she went out.

Nora was probably a target. Hell, even Meadow and her siblings might be too, given their connection to the vampire Dark Lord.

Meadow's heart rate kicked up, and she took deep breaths, wanting to avoid a panic attack. After breathing in for four, out for eight, and doing it a few times, the creeping sense of panic faded a little.

Helena said softly, "I can see we've upset you. We should send for your brother."

"No, no, I'll be fine. River's busy, and anxiety and panic attacks are something I've dealt with before. Nora mentioned she might have some special herbal tea to help, and I'll get it from her after you leave."

After studying her for a second, Helena replied, "If you're sure." Meadow nodded, and the other female continued, "Nadia will be back tomorrow afternoon. That way you can enjoy your night with your handsome vampires and not worry about being sleep-deprived for your first lesson." She paused, and then added, "And maybe if you end up marrying them, more fae witches can visit their pleasure house. I've always wondered about it myself. Maybe my fated lord is right there waiting for me."

Meadow frowned. "But fae witches don't have fated ones."

"No, but I've always wondered about a vampire's bite. Or a shifter's stamina. And they both have fated ones."

Nadia laughed. "Don't mind Helena. The male she

nearly married was a bastard. The day before her wedding, she learned he wanted her to be a second wife. Something he'd never mentioned before, either. Let's just say Helena wasn't happy about it."

Helena smiled slowly, with a glint in her eye. "He tried to run and hide, but I found him. I can find any fae witch in this country."

Meadow snorted. "That's definitely a handy power to have, if someone screws you over. Er, I mean does something bad to you."

"Screws you over," Helena repeated. "I like that one. I'll have to add it to my future vocabulary dictionary. Thank you."

"You're welcome?"

Helena bobbed her head. "Right, well, we should be off. I'll be back in a week to check on you and see if you need any other assistance."

Nadia waved a hand. "I'll be back tomorrow at 3 p.m. And if they have any more of those little cakes, I'd love to have them again with tea."

"I'll see what I can do."

Once they had said their goodbyes, Meadow shut the door and leaned against it.

While, yes, her head was filled with a lot of new information, mixed with a little anxiety, she was hopeful. She hadn't had any friends since high school—except for her mentor, but even that hadn't been super close, given the age difference—and while it was early days, she liked both Nadia and Helena.

It might've taken her traveling over a hundred years

into the past to find a place where she might, just might, fit in.

Don't get ahead of yourself, Meadow.

No, she needed to start learning more about this time and place, and quickly. So she headed upstairs and went through the small trunk. Hours flew by as she sorted through it and eventually wrote in her journal. By the time a package from Laurie and Joseph finally arrived, she was more than ready for a break.

After opening the box, she stared and then touched the material reverently. Tonight should be memorable, that was for sure.

And she couldn't wait.

Chapter Eleven

As the heads of security for Nyx's Kingdom, Frank Doyle and Susanna Rowe, finished giving their daily report, Laurie barely resisted looking at the clock for the tenth time.

Meadow should arrive at any minute, and he wondered if she'd ask for him and Joseph. He hoped so, but as impulsive as he usually was, Joseph had convinced him to hold back for the night. Otherwise, Meadow might run away and never return.

Frank cleared his throat. Laurie focused back on the vampire male and said, "I caught most of it, I promise. There was a scuffle between a shifter and a vampire, another between two humans, and a shifter tried to force her way inside. Nothing out of the ordinary for a busy night."

Frank grunted. "Right, but you also asked me to keep an ear out about the fae witch territory, and word on the street says a few more fae witches went missing this week."

Damn. It was a good thing Joseph was busy with the books and writing out order requests. The male was still upset over Meadow's revelations the night before, and Laurie had only managed to calm him down earlier in the day. The last thing he needed was for Joseph to get worked up again.

Not that Laurie would keep the news from Joseph for long, but just until after Meadow's visit. Because while he might know Joseph's moods and how he didn't anger easily under usual circumstances, Meadow might think differently and form an opinion that would be difficult to change.

The second head of security, Susanna, spoke up. "If you're worried about Miss Vale visiting, don't be, Laurie. We've double-checked the perimeter, have extra security inside, and two of the older teenage boys will be keeping an eye out for anything suspicious. She'll be safe here."

Laurie forced a smile. "I know, Susanna. You and Frank are the best there is, and had better be, given how much we pay you."

She rolled her eyes. "Yes, yes, we're expensive. But we *are* worth it. After all, since we've taken over security there's never been a serious incident inside Nyx's Kingdom. Proof is in the pudding."

After a few more minutes of conversation, he dismissed the pair and tried to concentrate on the upcoming event schedule. Their patrons paid handsomely for their memberships and wanted more than empty rooms to fuck on demand. Costumes, themes, and even consensual auctions for a night of fun were what made their place stand out in London.

Normally, he loved this part of his job. One month could feature Roman centurions and goddesses, another might be a mock court from Henry VIII, or another might have several masquerade balls. And since Laurie was the creative one while Joseph was the numbers and business one, their partnership had worked out well and become extremely profitable.

But now? Laurie lacked the fire to plan a new event. No, instead he kept remembering how he and Joseph had held Meadow between them the night before. Or how he'd carried her soft, warm body to her bed and how much he'd wanted to stay and hold her.

At least now he and Joseph understood a little better about why she had so little self-confidence, and he wanted to help restore it. Him and Joseph both.

However, that required being around Meadow, and she might not ask for them once she arrived. Not seeking her out would be bloody difficult. He'd do it because they needed to earn her trust, but it'd be one of the hardest things he'd done in a while.

I now better understand Leo's instinct around Yesenia, back in the early days, right after she blooded him. It'd been fun to tease his older brother at the time. And no doubt Leo would start doing the same to him.

Just as Laurie tried to focus on his next big ball, someone knocked. After bidding them to enter, one of the runners used to convey messages between the staff entered and shut the door. Laurie waved for him to speak, and the male said, "Miss Vale is here and asked for you and Mr. Hope."

"Thanks, Jimmy. I'll find Joseph and we'll meet her. Where is she?"

"The hidden viewing room off the large voyeur room."

Ah, so she'd decided to peek from behind a wall. He'd suspected she would, and that could work in his and Joseph's favor. "Thank you. You may return to your post."

The younger male dashed off, and Laurie straightened his tie and shirtsleeves before brushing back his hair. A quick check in the mirror showed he was put together, and he went off to find Joseph, smiling the entire way.

Meadow had asked for them. And maybe, just maybe, she'd ask them to help her find her release, too. Because the regular foursome tonight never held back, and no doubt, she'd be desperate by the end of their playtime.

MEADOW READJUSTED her mask for the tenth time as she waited inside a small room containing only a few chairs and a side table with refreshments. Well, and a wall with various closed slits in it.

When she'd first knocked on the main door, she'd

been nervous. But rather than the two male and two female guards intimidating her, they'd surprised her by being nice yet firm. Not to mention one of the females had even given Meadow a once-over, winking at the end before saying, "Too bad you blooded the bosses, Miss. We could've had some fun."

Meadow's cheeks had heated as the guards teased the one who'd spoken and told her to behave.

It wasn't as if she were wearing a super revealing dress or anything. It was all black, with long sleeves and a tight-fitting bodice that flared and billowed out from just under her breasts. However, it didn't go all the way to the floor, like most of the skirts and dresses she'd seen on everyday people; it stopped just above her knees. Along with the dress, Laurie and Joseph's package had included a diamond tiara and knee-high black boots. Not with heels, thankfully, and wearing them made her feel a little badass.

And almost pretty, too.

A knock made her jump—she really needed to stop doing that since she'd known people were coming—and she cleared her throat before saying, "Enter."

Joseph entered first but stopped as soon as his eyes met hers. Then he looked down her body, slowly, and back up. His eyes were heated, and Meadow nearly licked her lips.

"Move, Joseph."

Laurie entered and shut the door. As his eyes met hers, his smile died and his jaw dropped before his gaze took her in, pausing at her breasts, and finally met her eyes again. "You look bloody amazing, Meadow. I knew our usual place would do a good job, but damn."

Her cheeks flushed, and she glanced between Joseph and Laurie. Only when her hand went to her training bracelet did she finally smile at them. Their reactions weren't because of her magic. And yes, they could be acting. But she'd looked discreetly at their crotches when they'd checked her out, and both were aroused.

Was it solely because of her? Or from something they'd been doing just before coming here?

Before she could doubt herself yet again, they both walked over and each took a hand before kissing one of her cheeks. Joseph was the first to speak. "You look beautiful, Meadow. Do you like the dress? Laurie is better at fashion than me, and helped design this outfit."

They'd both stepped back and released her hands, sadly. But she managed to keep from fidgeting and replied, "I love it. I wasn't sure at first, as I don't like to show my legs. But it's just so pretty and goes really well with the boots."

Laurie grinned. "The boots definitely make the outfit shine. Well, after you, of course. Clothes should help bring out the best of a person, and this dress shows off your curves and beautiful legs."

Just as she was about to tell him that was hard to believe, a gong-type sound came from behind the wall with the viewing slits.

Joseph replied in a low voice, "That's the two-minute warning gong. The four members tonight should be entering and will start soon. Let me get you a glass of wine whilst Lauric sets up your chair in front of the viewing slit you want."

"Y-you're sure they want us to watch?"

Joseph nodded as he poured the wine. "Some people become more aroused knowing others are watching. This foursome, in particular, really loves it. They consist of two shifters and two vampires, which means it can last a long time and feature a lot of orgasms, depending on how often one of the vampires grazes someone's skin."

She glanced at one of Joseph's fangs and wondered what that would feel like, but quickly pushed the thought aside. Tonight was about seeing how others enjoyed having sex and could orgasm without magic, and nothing else.

Although, as Laurie motioned toward a center slit and grinned, showing off his fangs, she wondered if it was possible to have two vampires bite her at the same time. Would that cause a mega-orgasm? Or would it kill her?

"I know Joseph said for you to pick, but this one has the best view. And if you're comfortable with it, Joseph and I can sit to either side of you as well, and we can all watch together."

She blinked. "I never would've imagined that one day I'd be doing this—about to watch group sex with two vampires sitting on either side of me."

Laurie winked. "You didn't even mention the 1890 part, either."

She laughed. "No, that would've been even more of a fantasy, for sure."

He gestured. "Come, my lady. Your seat awaits."

She couldn't help smiling as Laurie assisted her to her seat. Once settled, he bowed. "If my lady wishes for anything else, she only has to ask."

Joseph walked over and handed out the wine glasses before saying, "If you encourage him, he'll only get worse. He can be a cheeky bastard."

Laurie put on a mock expression of hurt. "And here I thought you liked me."

Joseph rolled his eyes, and Meadow couldn't help but giggle.

Laurie looked back at her. "I love your laugh. I think I'll keep it up, so I can hear it as many times as possible."

Before she could reply, another gong sounded. Joseph nodded toward the slit in front of her. "Ready?"

After sipping her wine, and before she could change her mind, she quickly bobbed her head. Joseph slid open the ten-inch by about four-inch slit. She started leaning forward, but Joseph murmured, "Just a second."

Then his fingers went to the back of her head, and she could feel him undoing the mask ties. Once done, he pulled it away and placed it on the table. "You can put it back on later. But for now, it'll be easier to see."

She was vaguely aware of Laurie and Joseph sitting to either side of her, but her heart thudded as she finally looked through the opening in the wall.

On the other side was a large room, with a bed on a

slightly raised platform and chairs to either side, some full and some empty. However, the bed was huge, like two king-sized ones put together, and next to it, two males and two females were taking off their robes. To her surprise, they weren't all thin or super toned, but rather included a range of body types. And once naked, each person climbed onto the bed.

The rest of the tasteful, old-timey decor faded away as she watched one female kiss the other female, all while a male spread her thighs and lowered his head. The second male went behind the first and started running a fang along the side of his neck.

Meadow almost didn't know where to look as things moved quickly. The female on the bed didn't have fangs and had to be the shifter, while the vampire female now sat on the other female's face and moaned.

Meadow's eyes then darted to the two males, and the vampire behind the male was already running his cock along the other male's ass as he leaned over to kiss the vampire female.

She had no idea how they coordinated themselves, but it wasn't long before one male was thrusting into the shifter female on the bed. He now kissed the female over the other female's face, as the male behind him thrust inside him.

Everyone was moaning and groaning and breathing hard. And it went on and on, with various people changing positions, equally excited about each and every partner.

And one by one, they orgasmed. Sometimes together, sometimes on their own. And multiple times.

All without the use of magic.

As some of the onlookers inside the room started undressing and having sex as well, Meadow leaned back. Her heart thundered, and her core pulsed.

Never in a million years would she have thought she'd want to see a live show like that.

Oh, she could never have sex in front of an audience herself. But something about the mixture of lust and tenderness and love between the four people on the bed had both made her yearn for that herself and wish she were the type of person to just jump into bed with near-strangers.

Because in reality, Laurie and Joseph were exactly that.

Joseph whispered into her ear. "Well, what did you think?"

Even though all the slits were now closed, she whispered back, "You swear that was all without magic?"

His hot breath caressed her ear, and she shivered as he murmured, "No magic. It was all them. I vow it on Laurie's life."

Then Laurie whispered into her other ear, "Is there anything you need from us, pet? Just say the word, and we'll grant it."

She swallowed, needing a second to form a reply. Because the mixture of Laurie and Joseph's heat and scent made her squeeze her thighs together. Part of her wanted them to make her moan and groan just like the four people had in the other room.

And yet, she didn't know the vampire males. The

last time she'd tried to hook up with someone too soon, he'd been harsh and destroyed her confidence.

Joseph said, "Let us help you, Meadow. Even if you merely want a selection of toys to play with and orgasm on your own, that's fine. But you need some release. Don't deny yourself."

The idea of Victorian sex toys made her smile. But then Laurie's voice garnered her attention again. "What do you want, Meadow? Tell us. As long as it's not another male, we'll find it for you."

She played with the hem of her skirt, which sat about four inches above her knee now that she was sitting down.

What would it feel like to have either of their warm hands on her? Or, even, both of them at the same time?

At the thought of two males stroking between her thighs, Meadow pressed her legs even closer together. That was a dream, and nothing else. No male ever did something like that without wanting a blowjob or something in return.

And she'd been horrible at it before, according to her ex.

What if he'd been lying?

Laurie and Joseph coming into her life had made everything confusing, and she no longer knew who or what to believe.

Joseph moved his head until he caught her eye, and she sucked in a breath at the heat and desire in his gaze. Was that from the free show they'd watched?

Or maybe, just maybe, it was because of her?

No, that can't be. She still wore her training bracelet.

"Meadow," he stated, and she met his gaze again before he continued, "When we said we'd offer you anything, we meant it. I will absolutely honor your request, although do you want to know what I hope you ask for?"

She swallowed before asking, "What?"

He moved his hand until it hovered a few inches above her knee. As ridiculous as it was, she felt his heat.

Joseph spoke again, "Our touch. Just our hands, for now. But making you cry out will make me happy. Make both of us happy. Will you let us, Meadow? Will you let us give you some release?"

Before she could stop herself, she blurted, "Just your hands and nothing else?"

"For now, yes. I promise."

Laurie also moved into her field of vision. "I also promise. Just one hand from each of us, unless you ask for more."

For a few beats, she glanced between them. She wanted to scream, "Yes!" However, what if she couldn't orgasm without her magic or a vibrating toy? Would they get upset, say hateful words, and storm off?

Laurie murmured, "Won't you leave the past in the past for a short while, Meadow? You're beautiful, and desirable, and just the thought of touching your soft skin makes me hard. Nothing about you will disappoint me. Or us."

"You could never disappoint me, Meadow," Joseph said. "You're so bloody beautiful in that dress, and I'll be dreaming of you later. But for now, just remember that we're not those arseholes who hurt you before. Let us show you a little pleasure, all whilst you keep your training bracelet on."

After another deep breath, she glanced at each in turn. Could she really do this and risk being disappointed or berated later? They were both so sexy, and it would be like a dream come true. But only if it differed from her past experiences.

Maybe she should do the safe thing and say no.

And yet, would she regret it if she refused them?

Yes, yes she would.

So she nodded and blurted, "Okay. But don't say I didn't warn you, in case I disappoint you."

Joseph's jaw tightened a second before softening. "Can we also kiss your mouth?"

"I-I guess so."

"Yes or no, Meadow. I want you to be sure."

Her eyes moved to Joseph's full lips, and she licked her own. "Yes."

"Good."

Joseph took her lips in a rough kiss before she opened and let in his tongue.

He explored and tasted and lapped, and she slowly widened her thighs, needing more than a kiss.

Joseph broke the kiss, and she nearly cried out. However, he replied, "I will be tasting your sweet mouth again later, I promise. But I want to watch your face as we make you fall apart."

He and Laurie both placed a hand on a bare knee, and at their heat, a rush of desire shot through her.

Laurie rubbed the inside of her thigh while Joseph

ran his up and down the top of her other one. Joseph's hand was a little rougher, and Laurie's a bit softer. But as they continued teasing her skin and staring into her eyes, her clit pulsed. She needed more, so much more.

The corner of Laurie's mouth kicked up. "Tell us what you want, pet, and we'll give it to you."

He ran his hand closer to where her thigh met her core—she now understood why there hadn't been any sort of underthings with the dress—but stopped short of touching her where she ached for him. For them both.

She closed her eyes, and they both stilled their hands. She cried out and opened them again. "Why did you stop?"

Laurie shook his head. "Don't close those beautiful eyes, Meadow. Let us watch you enjoy our touch. Say the word, and we'll make it happen."

Her entire body ached for more than their hands—more touches, more kisses, and more skin-to-skin contact.

However, she wasn't ready for that. Not yet. She still didn't know if they would promise something and then leave her frustrated later. It wouldn't be the first time.

Joseph spoke up. "Focus on us, on now, and your body's needs, Meadow. Leave everything else outside that door."

Despite knowing the pair for such a short time, it seemed as if Joseph could read her thoughts and doubts already. How, she didn't know.

And it was a little unsettling.

Just as her mind started going down another rabbit hole, both vampires started caressing her legs again. She gasped as their touches made her skin tighter, hotter, and she ached. So much.

All she had to do was ask them to ease it.

Her voice was breathless to her own ears as she said, "Touch me."

Laurie quirked an eyebrow. "Where?"

She nearly shouted that they already knew where. And yet, she knew they needed her explicit words and consent. "My pussy."

Laurie smiled. "Ah, yes. That's what River calls it." His finger moved ever closer to her center. "Spread your legs wider and push up your skirts. I want to see your pretty cunny."

She hesitated because that would mean displaying her thighs too. However, Joseph cupped her inner thigh and squeezed before murmuring, "These are perfect, Meadow. I can't wait to one day have you press them against my head as I devour your sweet honey. Show us your beautiful pussy, as you call it."

With both of their hands so close, her core throbbed as her heart pounded. And after glancing at each vampire—they both stared at her skirt with anticipation—she finally gathered the material and drew it to her waist.

They both groaned as they pushed her thighs even further apart.

Laurie growled. "So fucking perfect."

"Are we really this lucky to have such a beautiful female blood us both?" Joseph asked.

She nearly told them to stop lying, but then one of them stroked her center as the other circled around her clit. Moaning, she arched into their touch, which was far too soft.

Joseph said, "Don't hold back. Your sounds and moans and movements will tell us what you like."

"Or, you can command us, pet, and we'll do as you say," Laurie added.

Unable to meet their eyes, she looked down at their hands. Joseph's lightly stroked her center, while Laurie circled her clit without ever touching it.

Just watching their hands made her hotter and wetter.

And yet, their soft touch would never get her over the finish line.

Joseph lightly thrust his finger inside her, and she gasped and arched into his touch. As he lazily stroked, she wished the stool had a back because she was in danger of falling off.

Laurie removed his hand, and she wanted to ask why. But then Joseph found a spot inside her and teased, and she forgot about everything else.

At least until she felt Laurie at her back, one arm going around her waist as the other went back between her legs. As he lazily circled her, he nuzzled her neck. "I hear your heart racing, Meadow. Normally, I'd want a little taste of your blood. But this first time, you're going to orgasm with our touch, and nothing else." He moved to her ear and whispered, "Remember, tell us what you want, pet. Let us help you find *la petite mort*."

Meadow had no idea what the last part meant, but

as Joseph leaned over to kiss her while Laurie kissed her neck, she forgot about everything except their touches and Joseph's taste, and the slowly building tension.

Joseph broke the kiss, and Laurie turned her head and took her lips. As he continued to explore and tangle with her tongue, Joseph added a second finger. Laurie continued circling her clit, and she needed a little more. Just a bit.

Once he broke the kiss, he stared into her eyes and said, "Ask for it, pet. Now."

Even though she knew Laurie was pure vampire and didn't have the fae witch power of persuasion, she felt like she had to answer. So she said, "Touch my clit a little harder, while you both take turns kissing me."

Laurie smiled as he moved his finger to finally stroke her, and she jerked. But he leaned away to allow Joseph to kiss her again, all while Laurie pressed and circled her bundle of nerves. Joseph never let up his thrusting fingers, and she was close.

Then Joseph moved his mouth to the corner of hers, and Laurie kissed her opposite corner. And as they both nuzzled her cheek and kissed part of her lips—with theirs touching at times too—the pressure built. Then Laurie pinched her, and she cried out as wave after wave of pleasure shot through her. Joseph never let up his fingers, and neither did Laurie, and it stretched on and on until she thought it might kill her.

But eventually they gentled their fingers while they also took turns kissing her. When she finally slumped against Laurie behind her, she struggled to keep her eyes open.

Joseph removed his fingers, raised one toward Laurie, and maintained eye contact as the other male sucked it into his mouth and moaned. Once Joseph removed it, he put the second finger into his own mouth and groaned as he licked it clean.

Maybe if she weren't so boneless right now, she'd feel embarrassed. However, because she was so tired, she only recognized one thing—vampires couldn't lie. Which meant if they seemed to enjoy her taste, there had to be some truth to it.

After Joseph wiped his hand with a handkerchief, he cupped her cheek. "Your training bracelet is still on, and I felt your greedy pussy gripping and releasing my fingers. You orgasmed, Meadow, and without your magic or a vampire's bite."

Laurie nuzzled her cheek. "I hope we've earned a little of your trust tonight, pet."

Between the warmth of Laurie at her back and Joseph gently rubbing his thumb up and down her cheek as he cupped it, a sense of peace settled over her.

However, doubt crept in, and she couldn't help wondering if this was all an act so they could claim her sooner.

Stop it, Meadow. If you only ever doubt them, especially after fulfilling their promise, you might destroy something before it ever starts.

And as crazy as it was, she wanted to give them a chance. She didn't fully trust them, and might never do so. But just the possibility of having a connection with someone—or two—after so many years alone was strong, and she yearned for a little closeness. Her siblings were here, of course. And yet, she wanted something more, something separate.

Finally, she replied, "You've earned a little bit of trust with me, yes."

Joseph asked, "So that means you'll allow us to woo you?"

It was such an old-fashioned term, and she smiled. "I suppose so." Joseph opened his mouth, and she added, "I mean yes."

He smiled, making the male even more handsome, if that were possible.

Laurie hugged her closer against him as he said, "That means we have a chance, and I intend to do my best to turn it into more."

If she weren't so tired, she might ask why he'd want to bother, given how he didn't really know her.

However, she yawned and struggled to keep her eyes open. Joseph scooped her into his arms and carried her to the door.

"Where are we going?" she asked.

"The corridor you used to get here is a secret one used for the staff, meaning we can take you to a more comfortable room down the hall without running into any of the patrons. There we can hold you as you nap, and when you wake up, you can decide if you want to see more or go home to your brother's house."

She should ask to go to River's place right now. She'd never been able to sleep with another person in the room. Well, apart from her siblings.

However, as she snuggled against Joseph's warm,

solid chest, she didn't have the energy to protest. She murmured, "Okay."

She was dimly aware of entering a room and Joseph sitting down on the couch. Soon she felt Laurie's arms go around them both.

And in less than a minute, warm and cozy with two males holding her, she fell fast asleep.

Chapter Twelve

As Joseph held Meadow in his lap, with Laurie sitting behind them on the sofa and engulfing them both in his arms, a sense of peace and longing shot through him. Even if Meadow was still clothed, and neither of them had tasted her sweet blood or thrust inside her, he wanted more of this. The three of them sharing and giving and taking, and afterward, holding each other and being surrounded by love.

Well, he hoped he and Laurie could win over Meadow's love. Because Joseph, at least, was falling for the sweet, damaged female who had more fire inside her than she probably realized.

And not just because she was their fated one, either. He believed in her, and once she realized she was finally free of her father and learned how to control her magic, she would be magnificent.

And she should be theirs.

He tightened his hold on her, and Meadow

snuggled closer against him. One of Laurie's hands stroked Joseph's cheek as the other stroked Meadow's side, and he murmured, "She's starting to trust us a little."

"Hmm." He leaned his head back on Laurie's shoulder before replying, "I wish we could help with her magic lessons as well, even though I know we can't."

Laurie chuckled. "You're one of the cleverest people I know, Joseph, but I think becoming a magic-less magic teacher would be a bit difficult. But there's no need to worry—Yesenia and River will ensure she's taught well and learns to embrace her powers. They're both fierce in their own ways, and given how they managed to win over Leo and Nora, that alone makes them extraordinary."

He grunted. "I know, but I like to be in charge of things."

Laurie leaned his cheek against the top of Joseph's head. "You do, and yet, you learned to trust me to handle half of the business. You'll come to trust her, too, and that will take time."

"And to think, I'm usually the patient one."

"Well, everyone can't be as perfect as me."

Joseph smiled as he gently elbowed Laurie behind him. "Don't start. Once you get going with your cheekiness, it can get out of control and you might wake her up."

Laurie sighed. "And that would be a bad thing?"

"She needs some sleep. Plus, I'm a bit selfish and want to hold her a little longer."

Laurie moved his hand to caress the side of Joseph's neck, up and down, sending a rush of heat through him. Laurie whispered, "I can't wait until we're both able to hold her in bed, naked, every night for the rest of our lives."

Laurie always fell in love fast. Sometimes it hurt him, and yet, Joseph was glad his lover was feeling the same about Meadow. Because the one time Laurie had fallen for their shared female but Joseph hadn't, it had been rocky.

But Joseph didn't think that would be a problem this time. Especially since Meadow leaned into his touch and asked for kisses. Unlike the female in their past, who'd tolerated him for Laurie's sake.

Pushing thoughts of the past to the side, he replied, "I hope for that, too, Laurie."

For the next few minutes, they remained silent. Joseph merely reveled in the warm, solidness of Laurie behind him and Meadow's softness in his lap. He wished they could sit like this for hours.

Except it would have to end, eventually. Meadow was nowhere near ready to stay the night with them.

After moving one hand to Laurie's thigh, Joseph asked, "Do you think Dark Lord Khan would allow us to take her to the Autumn celebration in the fae witch territory next month?"

The fae witches, at least in the UK, celebrated the changing seasons with big gatherings full of stalls and shows and even dances. Since the former vampire Dark Lord, Laurie's father, had been at war most of the time with the fae witches, Joseph had never attended a seasonal gathering before.

However, ten years ago, the fae witches, vampires, and shifters in London had formed a truce and signed a treaty. The fae witches were still wary, though, around the vampires. After all, Laurie's father had kidnapped and imprisoned and even tortured many of them decades before.

Hatred and fear were hard things to overcome in the best of times.

Laurie grunted. "Maybe, provided Leo and Yesenia, as well as River and Nora, accompany us. The fae witches have grown fond of River already, given his medical practice. And Yesenia has helped some of them with easy requests to find lost items, like treasured heirlooms or mementos. Maybe having them with us will keep some of the fae witches from thinking we'll instantly kill or kidnap them."

He rubbed Laurie's thigh, which had tensed. Laurie's father had made all of his children's lives hell, in their own way, on top of what he'd done to the fae witches. Laurie often carried guilt for not only being unable to help their former allies but also for not being able to rescue his sister.

With his huge heart, Laurie would try to save the world if he could.

It was one of the many things he loved about him.

Joseph said, "Well, then we'll ask your siblings if they'd like to go to the festival. I'm sure they'll say yes since Leo wants to mend things with the fae witches, given his wife. We'll just need to be on our guard if

Khan says we can attend, in case the French vampires try something. We'll either need permission to take some of our own guards, or ask Dark Lord Khan for some extra eyes."

Meadow sighed and leaned more heavily against Joseph. He leaned up and kissed her forehead before resting back against Laurie again. He added, "We'll ask Meadow first to see if she wants to go before we plan anything. After so many years in hiding, maybe she doesn't want to face the crowds."

Joseph might've fended for himself on the streets of London, but he'd been used to living among massive amounts of people. The future sounded a bit more isolating, and maybe it wasn't what Meadow wanted.

Laurie replied, "We'll ask, but I think she isn't a recluse by nature, only by necessity."

"I get that sense as well."

"Then let's make sure to ask her about it before we take her home."

Joseph grunted, and they fell quiet again. Soon he heard Laurie softly snoring behind him. Joseph stayed awake, though, and made plans on how to convince Meadow to go to the fae witch festival with them, as well as dreaming of a day when Laurie wouldn't carry guilt for his father's sins any longer.

Chapter Thirteen

The next day, Meadow tried for the tenth time to stop replaying events from the night before.

She'd dreamt all night of Laurie and Joseph, their hands and mouths, and how she'd orgasmed the hardest in her life. And even if afterward was a little fuzzy, she remembered waking up in Joseph's lap, with Laurie hugging an arm around them both, one of them softly snoring behind her.

She'd actually kept her breathing even and had remained still for a little while, wanting to absorb the situation and how it made her feel. Instead of being embarrassed or overwhelmed, she'd actually wondered what sharing a bed with them would be like.

Was one of them a bed hog? Or, did they like their space? Would they ever cuddle with her? Of course, maybe Laurie and Joseph would just sleep close together and leave her alone.

But no, she didn't like that last scenario. At all. She wanted both of them close.

Which was strange, since she'd never wanted another male, let alone two, to sleep in the same bed as her. Maybe it'd been a one-off, because of her orgasm.

And yet, she'd never felt as comfortable with new people as she had with Laurie and Joseph. Meadow was in new territory, and that didn't even include the whole being-in-the-past thing, either.

Sadly, before she'd figured anything out at all, Joseph had noticed she was awake, and she'd made excuses to go home. Which, of course, she regretted since she'd secretly wanted to see more of Nyx's Kingdom.

However, they'd been gentlemen and saw her home straight away.

Well, mostly gentlemen. They'd both given her searing goodnight kisses.

Stop replaying it all, Meadow. Nadia will be here soon, and you need to focus. If you can't learn to control your magic and monetize it, you'll always be a burden.

Her siblings would argue that point, saying she could never be a burden. But years of her father saying that the potential of her magic was the only reason he hadn't shipped her off to one of her relatives—separating her from her siblings—had taken its toll.

Pushing aside thoughts of her father, Meadow did some rhythmic breathing. And by the time someone knocked on the door, she had calmed down and was ready for her magic lessons.

Nadia entered, carrying a satchel. "Good morning, Meadow. How did last night go?"

For a second, she hesitated. Meadow wasn't used to sharing things with people. And yet, if she wanted to try making friends in this time period, she needed to open up a little. So, she forced herself to reply, "Good. Better than I thought."

Nadia sat down across from her and quirked an eyebrow. "Does that mean you ended up in bed with them both?"

"Er, not exactly." She bit her bottom lip and then added, "But let's just say they can be rather convincing when they put their minds to it."

Nadia chuckled. "That doesn't surprise me. And not just because you're their fated one, either. They've somehow been given permission to attend the Autumn Festival next month, and no vampire has attended in a long, long time. Half-vampires, yes, but they were still part fae witch. But the notice came from Dark Lord Khan's office, so it must be true."

Meadow frowned. She vaguely remembered Laurie and Joseph asking if she wanted to attend and saying yes. But she'd thought it some trivial thing.

She really needed to learn more about this time period and all the rivalries, wars, and so forth.

She asked, "Why would Dark Lord Khan send out a magical alert to everyone about them attending?"

"Well, the more time we have to get used to the idea, the better, given the past between the vampire and fae witch territories in London. Some of the hotter heads are plotting revenge for dead ancestors, but Dark

Lord Khan has time to sort them out. I may not agree with or understand everything he does, but I do think we need to start banding together with the shifters and vampires instead of fighting amongst ourselves."

Looking down at her lap, Meadow twisted her fingers. "It's my fault he has to do any of that, isn't it? But I don't want to cause any trouble, and I can get them to cancel."

"No, don't."

She met Nadia's gaze again. "No?"

She shook her head. "No. We've been allies with the vampires for nearly a decade now, and we need to start making changes beyond a written treaty. Besides, Dark Lord Yates will be attending with Yesenia, and Dr. Vale with Nora. For most fae witches, having two Dark Lords at the festival will be a massive deal. Even more so if the shifter Dark Lord, Everett Black, attends as well. And he might."

"But will they be safe? I don't want River or Yesenia, or anyone else for that matter, getting hurt because of me."

"Extra security had already been planned, given all the recent kidnappings. There had been talk of canceling the festival, but it's been going on for nearly two hundred years—even when we were at war with the vampires, albeit it was much smaller then—and the fae witches can be stubborn. Maybe not as much as the shifters, but we're close."

She winked, and some of Meadow's anxiety faded. "So you'll be attending?"

"Of course, along with my husband and my

daughter. My brother will be running a stall, too, so you'll need to stop by and say hello."

"I'll try. Everything will be new to me, and while it's probably impossible, I want to see as much of it as I can. If nothing else, it'll help my brain fully accept that I am in 1890 and not in some kind of strange dream."

"Good. The more accustomed you get to London and this time, the better. I suspect it'll make your magic easier to control, too, if you feel more at home."

Home. No place had really felt like home since her mother's death. Oh, Yesenia and River had tried their best. However, their father had always been there, and since Meadow was the youngest, she'd had to live with him the longest without the others.

Maybe this time and place would become her home.

No, don't get your hopes up. Things could still go wrong. Not wanting to dwell and get anxious, she changed the subject. "So, what are we going to do today?"

Thankfully, Nadia didn't blink at the change of topic. "We're going to test how much control you have over your magic."

She swallowed. "We are? How?"

"I brought a volunteer with me. He's waiting in the hall, for when you're ready."

Meadow's hand went to her training bracelet. "B-but what if I can't control my powers at all?"

"I would never put you or anyone else in danger, Meadow, I promise. I can always put your training bracelet back on. Besides, he's half fae witch and half human, which is one of the hardest types to influence with our magic."

"He's half human and half fae witch? But I thought they were incredibly rare."

Conception rates between humans and paranormals weren't great to begin with, but for some reason the rate was lowest between humans and fae witches. Meadow had only met one such individual in her life.

"It is, and he's one of the few in the UK. But in addition to him being harder to influence with magic, his research overlaps with our purposes. He's studying the effects of fae witch magic over different combinations of human, fae witch, vampire, and shifter, and trying to pinpoint which are the most susceptible and the least. Whilst we have guesses, he wants to document and get a definitive answer."

"And so he wants to use himself as a guinea pig?" At Nadia's confused look, she rephrased. "That means he wants to be a test subject. Does that make sense?"

"Ah, yes, I understand now. And yes, he does. He often volunteers to help with magical training, and both sides benefit—our students are less likely to affect him, and he gets more data for his research. Dark Lord Khan is extremely interested in his work as well, as you can imagine." Nadia rearranged a few books on her lap and took out a small notebook and a pencil. "Since he's a busy person, could we get started? After he comes into the room, he'll sit near the fireplace, and you'll take off your bracelet. If things get out of control, I'll put your training bracelet back on."

And since Nadia had the same main power as Meadow, she would be highly immune to her magic. Not completely, but it would take a lot of power and focus to weave a spell over another fae witch who controlled lust and desire.

Meadow traced the edge of her training bracelet, knowing she needed to do this. And yet, after a few days of not having to worry about her magic and almost feeling normal, she was afraid of what might happen.

Nadia's voice was softer as she said, "He's fully aware of your magic, volunteered, and he's helped me train others before. I won't allow anything to get out of control, I promise. Even if it's early days, I need you to try trusting me, Meadow, or we'll never make any progress."

She glanced down at her training bracelet. "I know that. And yet, it's so hard for me. I-I just want to be normal. And I'm deathly afraid I'm not."

Nadia's hand covered hers, and Meadow looked up to see the fae witch bending over her. "You are normal, Meadow. Any fae witch that doesn't receive proper training would face challenges like yours. But I'm here to help, not to mention you also have Dark Lord Khan's support. So won't you at least try taking the bracelet off? Because if you're only ever afraid, you'll never make progress."

Maybe it was a little harsh, but Nadia was right. Even if Meadow had received almost no training after her powers had manifested at eighteen, one of the core fae witch tenets was that emotions had a big influence over magic. She'd kind of forgotten that over the years, but after several days of being reunited with her siblings and not having the constant fear of weaving magic over strangers, she'd started to recall some of her lessons. Even the books Nadia had lent her had briefly touched on the topic.

It would take time, of course, to not be constantly afraid of messing up. However, this was a controlled circumstance. If she couldn't seize this opportunity to learn, she might as well give up now.

No. She might've lost hope for a few years—when she'd thought her siblings were dead—but she'd never fully given up. Somewhere, deep inside her, she wanted to prove her father wrong. He'd repeatedly called her a failure, stupid, and a million other insults, and it'd affected her more than she'd thought.

But she would never have to see her father again. Plus, she had her siblings, as well as two vampires who made her feel at least a little attractive. Ones she secretly dreamed would want her past the claiming, and who would find her magic useful, meaning she'd feel less reliant on them or anyone else.

All she had to do was focus, and then maybe she'd become a badass fae witch, one with strong magic she could use on her terms. She just had to take this first step.

After taking a deep breath, Meadow nodded and said, "Okay, I'll do as you ask. Just please don't let me cause any chaos or harm."

Nadia patted her hand and stood upright. "I won't.

Now, before you take off your training bracelet, let me fetch our volunteer."

Meadow's heart thundered in her chest as she watched Nadia open the door and a man in his thirties walked in. He was of medium height, with blond hair and brown eyes, and wore the usual suit, tie, and waistcoat of this time period.

Since his hair was short, she could see the faintest points of his ears—far too subtle for any full fae witch, but definitely not round enough to be human.

As she wondered about his backstory, he bowed and spoke in the same British accent everyone else did around here. "Hello, Miss Vale. My name is Giles Dawson—please call me Giles—and thank you for allowing me to volunteer. I assume Mrs. Ahmed told you I'll be taking notes for my research?" Meadow nodded, and he continued, "Then let me just assure you that I will never use your true name and everything is kept confidential. My only goal is to better understand the intricacies of fae witch magic."

She blurted, "Did you inherit any?"

It wasn't common for a half-human to do so, but it wasn't impossible.

He smiled. "The only thing I can do is light candles, fireplaces, or stoves. I have fire magic, but only a fraction of what full-blooded fae witches can manage."

Meadow hesitated before asking, "And you know I control lust and desire? And there's a risk it might affect you?"

"Yes, I'm aware. However, as I'm sure Mrs. Ahmed

has explained, very few magical powers actually affect me. And if things get out of control, Mrs. Ahmed will take charge. I've worked with her before, so I trust her. Now, shall we get started? I don't wish to be rude, but I have some other appointments today and I want to make sure you have enough time to try out a few of Mrs. Ahmed's exercises."

"Um, okay. We can start."

With a nod, Giles went over to the fireplace and waited.

Nadia sat next to Meadow on the small sofa and said, "For this exercise, look at me, Meadow." She met her gaze, and the other female continued, "Before you remove the bracelet, tell me: have you learned any channeling exercises? Ones to help calm your mind and gather your magical power together, to draw on when needed?"

"Yes, when my magic first manifested. However, it's been a long time since I tried using them. Usually I just tried to contain my powers and only let them out when I was hired for a job. And in that case, I'd just let everything go and hope for the best."

"Well, let's start there, then. Imagine channeling and containing magical energy in your chest area, and then keep it there. While the bracelet won't allow the magic to flow out of you, you can still gather it together. So try that now, and let me know when you're done."

After a quick glance at Giles—who nodded in encouragement—Meadow closed her eyes.

In the past, she'd gathered magic as quickly as

possible, just wanting to get it over with. However, this time, with the bracelet on to stop it from escaping, she imagined it coming from her fingertips, toes, and head into her body, little by little, as the heat gathered in the center of her chest. Her magic had always glowed a slight red in the past, and so she imagined a ball of red energy swirling round and round. Once she had it contained and stable, she opened her eyes. "I've finished."

Nadia nodded. "Good. I'm going to remove the bracelet now, and I want you to reach out to Giles and try weaving it over him."

Her gaze moved to the male. "Are you sure?"

He replied, "Yes. If I feel anything, I'll let you know."

Nadia spoke again. "Since you have the secondary power of persuasion, today I want you to silently weave your magical net over him. We just want to judge your main power for today, and we can address the persuasion later." She placed her fingers over the bracelet. "Ready?"

She wanted to scream no, she wasn't. However, Meadow had been a coward for far too long, out of necessity, and she was determined to be braver about her magic going forward. "Yes."

"Right, then let's see what happens."

Nadia quickly removed her bracelet, and Meadow focused on Giles. In the past, she'd just roughly aimed her magic at the individuals who'd paid her. However, she wanted to try using more skill and finesse this time. So she slowly imagined threads of her magic flowing over to Giles, laying down over him, bit by bit, in a crosshatch pattern.

However, she'd barely gotten halfway through the task when Giles's eyes changed, zeroing in on her and then Nadia. He took a step forward before closing his eyes and putting his hands to his head. His voice was strained as he said, "Stop. You must stop, or I'll do something horrible."

As he took another step toward them, Nadia slid Meadow's bracelet on, and Giles dropped to his knees on the floor. Bracing his hands on the carpet, he breathed heavily.

Meadow stared in horror as Nadia rushed to his side and asked, "Are you okay, Giles? What happened?"

But before he said anything, Meadow understood. Her magic had been strong enough to influence one of the most magic-resistant beings on the planet.

She was not merely a fae witch with magic; she held one of the highest tiers—a Wielder.

A Wielder of Lust and Desire.

How could she ever learn to contain it?

Maybe she never would.

Her eyes heated with tears. It'd been foolish to hope she could be normal.

After placing a hand over her training bracelet, she stood. "I'm sorry. So, so sorry."

And then she rushed out of the room. Because no doubt, Giles and Nadia would look at her differently, say she couldn't be trained, and that she was a freak.

Just like her father had always said, when she'd

hidden away rather than use her magic as he'd asked her to do.

A few tears rolled down her cheeks as she rushed up the stairs to her room. Once inside, she shut and locked the door before sitting on the floor. She placed her head on her knees and cried.

Most fae witches would be ecstatic to have magic strong enough to influence anyone.

But to Meadow, it was her worst nightmare.

Because if she couldn't control it, she could be locked away. No doubt this time period had similar magical prisons for those with powerful-yet-unrestrained magic.

Yes, a bracelet could contain it. However, it was easy enough to slip off or be stolen.

Maybe this had been her chance, and now Dark Lord Khan would deem her too much work and lock her away.

She played out every worst-case scenario, and even though River and Nora tried to talk to her at some point, she told them to leave her alone.

For now, at least, she wanted to be by herself, wearing the training bracelet, and not worrying that she'd influence anyone to do something they didn't want to.

Chapter Fourteen

Later that day, Laurie stood with Joseph outside Meadow's bedroom.

Nora had written to him a few hours ago, explaining what had happened during Meadow's training session.

Apparently, she had unusually strong magic, the kind that could influence just about anyone.

And she hadn't taken it well.

Given what they'd learned about Meadow's father, and her fear of her powers, and all the rest, she probably expected to be shipped to the secret fae witch prison that everyone knew existed but had no idea where it was located.

Usually, only rogue fae witches who used magic for selfish or malicious reasons were imprisoned there. Yes, sometimes there was a fae witch with strong powers sent there, too, but only if they posed a major risk to society as a whole. And only if everything had been done to try and train them properly beforehand.

Meadow no doubt thought she was in the latter category. However, Nora had assured Laurie and Joseph that the female merely needed lessons and to stop being afraid of her own abilities. Her magic teacher had thought the same.

River had tried telling Meadow his thoughts, too, but she'd locked herself in her room, refusing to see anyone.

After receiving the letter from Nora, Laurie had wanted nothing more than to rush over and break down the door so he could comfort her. Joseph, on the other hand, had suggested they come up with a plan to help Meadow first.

Joseph's levelheadedness had prevailed, which was why they now stood in front of her door later in the day, ready to put their idea into action. After one more glance at Joseph, Laurie knocked.

Right away Meadow answered, "Go away. Please."

He cleared his throat before replying, "It's Laurie and Joseph, Meadow. And we need your help."

A pause and then she replied, "What kind of help?"

"Could we maybe talk face-to-face? I'd rather not shout our problem through a door and have it echo down the hallway."

He heard Meadow blow her nose and then say, "I look like crap right now. Can't you just tell me your problem this way?"

Joseph finally spoke up, but a little quieter. "It's killing me to hear you upset, love. Please let us in."

The fact that Joseph was being tender in public was a big deal, and Laurie resisted a smile.

However, he didn't think anyone could resist Joseph's tender tone—Laurie sure couldn't—and soon the door unlocked. Meadow opened it a few inches, and the sight of her red-rimmed eyes made him want to hold her, spoil her, and make her feel better in each and every way possible.

Her gaze darted between him and Joseph before she stepped back and widened the door.

He entered, with Joseph at his heels.

Once Meadow shut the door and turned toward them, Joseph reached out to cup her cheek, and Laurie took one of her hands in his.

She didn't try to tug or step away, which made hope flicker inside Laurie's chest. Maybe, just maybe, she was starting to trust them a little.

Well, and maybe like them, too. However, in the present, they needed to focus on Meadow and the fear of her magic.

Laurie squeezed her hand and asked, "What's wrong, pet? Yes, we truly do need your help. But something's upset you, and I don't like it."

Joseph grunted. "Me, either. Who made you cry?"

Meadow glanced to the side, but still didn't move away from their touches. She whispered, "Myself. I-I'm a Wielder, apparently. And it's only a matter of time before they toss me into prison."

Laurie might be a vampire, but every paranormal knew that to be classified as a wielder of anything meant a fae witch's magic was unusually strong. "Khan won't do that."

She frowned and met his gaze. "Why would you say that?"

"Well, first, your sister is married to the vampire Dark Lord, and Khan doesn't want to risk that alliance."

"But—"

Laurie cut her off. "And second, you've had what? One short magic lesson? It often takes a year or two for a fae witch to learn the intricacies of their powers. Next you'll say you're older and it's more difficult to learn, but Yesenia was also older when she started her magic lessons. And it took her over six months before she could do anything complex, and she still has a lot to learn. You just need time, Meadow, and to realize just how useful your powers can be."

She scoffed. "Useful if you don't want to take blue pills, maybe. But that's hardly changing the world."

Laurie replied, "I have no idea about these blue pills, but your type of magic is for more than fun or adventure—it can also genuinely help people. In fact, we want to ask you to help someone we know. Or, rather, he's the brother of one of the regular patrons, but he's still a good male who deserves some pleasure after what he went through."

She glanced between them. "What are you talking about?"

Laurie nodded at Joseph, since he knew the person in question better.

Joseph stroked his thumb on Meadow's cheek as he

said, "The person who needs your help is named Michael. He fought with the shifter unit of the British Army, at least until he was gravely injured a few years ago. While most of his injuries have healed, he's struggled to get an erection ever since. And one night, when he was in his cups, he told me he found his fated one and scented her orgasm. However, he can't fully claim her because..."

Meadow finished, "He needs to bite her as he orgasms to mark her."

Joseph nodded. "Exactly. He's seen every fae witch doctor he could, including your brother. However, none of them could help him, not even with magic-infused potions. Their last suggestion was to hire a fae witch with the power to control lust and desire. And since you have extremely strong magic, you're his best chance at being able to claim his fated one."

Laurie held his breath as Meadow glanced between them. He wanted her to accept their request and see that her magic could do good. Because a shifter who'd found their fated one but couldn't claim them would become overly protective, irritable, and even possessive. Sometimes it changed their personality completely, and if their fated one ran away without being marked, they could go insane, much like a vampire if they didn't bite and orgasm inside their fated bride or lord.

Meadow finally replied, "I want to help, but all I can do is unleash my magic without any kind of finesse. That was fine back home, since I was a super affordable fae witch for hire and they didn't expect anything more. However, from all I've heard from my former mentor, shifters want someone skilled for their claimings, and I can't do that."

Joseph smiled at her. "Trust me, Michael doesn't care about finesse. He wants to complete the claiming, and if successful, will continue to hire a fae witch to help with his problem in the future. Your brother said that after a while, he might not need magic. Especially if it's partially a mental block that keeps him from getting hard."

Given Laurie and Joseph's work, they spoke bluntly about sex. A lot of paranormals would scold them for doing so, but when Meadow didn't even blink at the mention, Laurie mentally sighed in relief. The last thing he wanted was to hold back with her.

Laurie squeezed Meadow's hand in his. "Will you use your magic to try to help him? We can clear out Nyx's Kingdom of anyone who doesn't have a magic-blocking ring or bracelet, and it'll be just us three, as well as Michael and his fated female. His brother has even offered to pay whatever it costs."

After looking to the side, she whispered, "But what if it all goes wrong? Or that I get so nervous that I mess it all up?"

Joseph moved his hand to the back of Meadow's neck and kneaded his fingers. Since Laurie had been on the receiving end of Joseph's skilled fingers, he wasn't surprised when Meadow's body softened a fraction.

Joseph said, "We can help you relax beforehand. And no, I'm not talking about orgasms, although those are always on offer. But if Laurie and I massage you, and give you wine, and make you less anxious, you'll probably worry less about doing something wrong and focus on merely unleashing your magic."

Taking his cue, Laurie began to massage Meadow's hand and fingers. She soon started moaning, and it took everything he had to keep his cock soft. As much as he wanted to be inside her, this was too important. Because his gut told him that if Meadow didn't take this first step, she might never break through her wall of fear and shame.

Eventually she pulled away, and they both let her walk to the side of the room. She wrung her hands a few seconds before saying, "I'll try. But I want you to tell him the truth about it being an amateur attempt at best."

Joseph nodded. "Of course. Since it'll take a few days, or maybe a week, to set it all up, will you meet with Nadia for more lessons until then?" Meadow opened her mouth to protest, but Joseph beat her to it. "She told River that your magic didn't affect her today, and she even offered to wear a magic-blocking ring like ours the next time, if it'll help you focus. However, she believes in you and sees your potential."

"But Dark Lord Khan…will he want to waste more time and resources on me?"

Laurie arched an eyebrow. "Why wouldn't he? Wielders aren't overly common, and that male has a web of plans I can't even begin to understand. If anything, he'll see you as another piece on his massive chessboard."

Joseph jumped in again. "Besides, he'd be a fool not to invest in you now, given how much you can charge in the future and be able to tithe to him later. Fae witches are quite mercenary about their powers, at times."

Laurie resisted rolling his eyes. Leave it to Joseph to bring in the business aspect of things.

However, it seemed to give Meadow the push she needed, and she stopped wringing her hands. "That's true. And I have to admit, I'd like to make enough to earn my keep and pay everyone back."

Part of him wondered if she was planning a future without him and Joseph, and Laurie wanted to haul her close and tell her she was theirs.

But he held back, aware that until Meadow was more comfortable with herself, she'd never trust her wants and desires. Ones that Laurie hoped included them as well.

Joseph nodded. "Right, then that's all settled. As soon as everything's in place, we'll send you a note. You should probably come to the pleasure house again before then, though, to get a feel for the place."

"I can go through the secret hallways again, right?"

Laurie replied, "Of course. Besides, it means we'll have you all to ourselves."

He winked, and Meadow's cheeks blushed. Just as he thought to tease her again, she yawned.

Given her busy day, she had to be exhausted. Teasing would have to wait.

The need to take care of her coursed through him, so Laurie strode over, swept her into his arms, and headed for the bed.

"What are you doing?" she asked.

"You're exhausted, pet. So I thought Joseph and I could help you relax before letting you get some sleep."

Her cheeks flushed even more. "Help how?"

The corner of his mouth kicked up. "Not that way. Not right now." He leaned over and whispered, "I want you awake when I finally make you come with my mouth."

"Oh."

Joseph chuckled, but Laurie replied to Meadow, "No, for now we're merely going to give you a massage and show you how we can help you relax for when you help Michael."

He nodded at Joseph, and the other male sat on Meadow's bed, with his back against the headboard. Laurie settled Meadow between Joseph's legs before pushing up her skirts to her knees.

She squeaked. "What are you doing?"

Joseph placed his hands on her shoulders and kneaded. Within seconds, she slumped against him. "Helping you to relax. We won't touch you like before, not tonight. But Laurie is famous for his foot massages."

She glanced at Laurie and then her feet. "Um, I've never had one of those before."

"Well, let's fix that, pet." He waited a beat to ensure she didn't refuse. When she merely nodded, Laurie removed her stocking—much quicker than he wanted—and then took her foot into his hands.

As he began pressing and kneading, Meadow moaned. "Oh, that's good. Both of you are way too good at this."

He smiled at her and shared a contented glance with Joseph before replying, "The benefit of me and Joseph knowing each other so long is that we know each other's strengths and weaknesses, meaning we know what we can do individually to make you feel the best."

She sighed contentedly. "I was worried about that, about you two being so close, but maybe it's not all bad."

Joseph whispered into her ear, "Laurie and I may be close, but you help bring out the best in both of us, love. You're the missing piece we've been waiting for."

"Mmm." Meadow's eyes were closed, and Laurie wasn't entirely sure she was listening.

In fact, she fell asleep a few minutes later. She didn't even wake up when they maneuvered her onto her back and got off the bed.

As he and Joseph stood watching Meadow, who looked so much younger in her sleep without her troubles weighing her down, he murmured, "I wish we didn't have to leave her."

Joseph took his hand and squeezed it. "Me, too. But we must take it slow with her, Laurie. I know it's not your favorite thing to hear, but it's the only way to win her for good."

He sighed and leaned his head on Joseph's shoulder. "I know." After another minute, he stood, and they headed out the door. Once they reached the downstairs corridor, River and Nora stopped them. But Laurie and Joseph merely told them that Meadow was asleep but had agreed to more magic lessons and to help them with a confidential problem.

River had tried to wheedle out more information, but they weren't about to reveal Michael's personal details, and so stood firm and revealed nothing.

By the time they reached their carriage and climbed inside, Laurie couldn't stop smiling. They'd been there to support Meadow, and now she trusted them a little. He also couldn't wait to see her expression when she helped Michael and started to see the value and impact of her powers in a positive light.

Chapter Fifteen

Over the next few days, Meadow met with Nadia and practiced gathering her magic, releasing it, and repeating the process until exhaustion set in. And by the fourth day, when Giles Dawson returned as a volunteer again, Meadow was able to temper how much magic she released and determine the limit where it started to affect Giles.

While she'd have to test out her limits further on those more susceptible to magic, it made her feel like she'd accomplished something. Because as well-meaning as Stacey had been, she hadn't possessed the patience to repeat exercises until Meadow found her "sweet spot" for weaving magic without exhausting herself.

Once she finished her most recent lesson and was alone for barely a minute, there was a knock and Yesenia entered, with Nora right behind her.

She stood and hugged her sister before asking,

"What are you doing here? I didn't expect you to visit today."

Yesenia waved a hand in dismissal. "It took some convincing before Leo said it was okay." She winked. "But he's easier to manage than you think."

Nora sighed. "That's my brother you're talking about."

Yesenia snorted. "Well, when you have three siblings matched with three siblings and one unrelated person, that's what's going to happen. I guess we can all drool over Joseph?" She glanced back at Meadow. "Have you seen him with his shirt off yet? He might be the quieter one of the pair, but sometimes the serious ones can surprise you."

Meadow fought a blush. "Er, no. Considering the last time I saw them I had puffy red eyes and snot coming out of my nose, they weren't exactly inspired to strip and seduce me. They've obviously stayed clear of me ever since."

Even to her own ears, she sounded irritated.

Nora smiled. "Only because Dark Lord Khan ordered them to, until this evening."

"Wait, what? Why would Dark Lord Khan order them to stay away? I thought I had free rein to see them."

"You were given permission to travel to the vampire territory, yes, but not the other way around," Nora replied. "And crossing the boundaries without an invitation is unwise, given the fear the fae witches still have surrounding vampires."

"Do they bully you, Nora?" Meadow demanded,

ready to stand up to anyone who mistreated her kind sister-in-law.

"No, no, not since the first few days. Between River and my own actions helping in the clinic, they've come to like or at least tolerate me."

Meadow huffed. "Still, if they ever say something mean, tell me."

"I will, although you'll have to stand behind River."

As Nora smiled fondly, Meadow's heart ached. Would she ever have that dreamy look on her face too about a male? Or, maybe, about two males?

Yesenia shook her head, interrupting her thoughts. "At any rate, for a fae witch, Khan definitely thinks like a vampire when it comes to language and negotiations or orders. You can tell he doesn't understand the pull of a fated one. Too bad he'll never have one himself."

"It's possible he ends up as one of a vampire or shifter, though," Nora stated.

Yesenia smiled deviously. "Hmm, there's an idea." She looked back at Meadow. "At any rate, do you want to see Laurie and Joseph? Laurie's been moping a bit lately—he's not as good at hiding his emotions as Joseph—and you could go to Nyx's Kingdom tonight. There's a masquerade ball, and while I'm close to convincing Leo to go to one, he's not quite there yet. But you could go and tell me about it, and then I can maybe use that to get my husband to say yes."

"So much for Leo being a super-powerful Dark Lord," Meadow drawled.

Yesenia smirked. "He is for everyone else."

Meadow laughed.

Nora spoke up. "So? Will you go then? Because if so, we'll help you get ready."

Meadow had been trying not to miss the vampire males, but had failed miserably. She'd hesitated about sending messages to them, certain they'd had enough of her problems, especially when it came to her magic.

Yesenia placed a hand on her shoulder and squeezed. "Both Laurie and Joseph are grumpier than usual, and it's because they haven't been able to see you. And before you say it's just the need to claim you, I think it's more." She paused, searched Meadow's eyes, and asked, "Isn't it?"

At one time, she'd told Yesenia almost everything.

However, during the three years when she'd believed her older sister had been dead, some of that closeness had faded. She wanted it back, and yet, she didn't want to disappoint Yesenia, who had sacrificed so much to help her and River.

Yesenia pulled her into a hug. "I'm sorry it took so long for me to get you here. If I'd only trained more and been a little more patient, I could've timed it better so that you came to us sooner. But I was desperate to have you safe, and it ended up causing you pain anyway."

She tightened her arms around her sister. "Rationally, I know that. And I forgive you, I promise you, I do. But it's going to take some time for me to really accept that you and River are alive and well, and that you didn't forget about me."

Yesenia squeezed and then leaned back to meet her gaze again. "As much as the older sister in me wants to demand you tell me everything, I understand and will try not to ask too often about Laurie and Joseph. But I will continue to ask, Meadow, because I want you to be happy, no matter what that means for you in this time." She hesitated and then asked, "I know it's only been about ten days since you arrived, but do you think you can be happy here? Eventually, I'll be skilled enough to send you back to the future. I don't want you to go, but I will do whatever you decide, I promise."

She smiled at her sister. "I think eventually I can be happy here. Between actual magic lessons, you and River, and my new friends like Nora and Nadia, I like it here. Well, most of the time. I have to admit I miss ebooks and the ability to check them out from the library and download them seconds later."

"Ah, yes, Wi-Fi. I missed it a lot more at first, but I've sort of gotten used to not having it. As long as I have hot water, a flushing toilet, and electric lights, I can handle this time period; luckily, my husband has the money for all those things. But as for your book problem, I know Leo has a giant library, as do Laurie and Joseph. The books might be a little more slow-paced, given the slower pace of life in general here, but there are still some good ones. Or, hey, maybe you could write a book and see what happens. Nothing that crosses the line about sharing future knowledge, but I'm sure people would read your stories. Females, in particular, could do with more books that have strong heroines."

She frowned. "I can't believe you remembered that I always wanted to write a book."

Yesenia nodded. "I know you stopped thinking about it once you got your magic, but without TV or the internet or even radio, you'll have a lot more time to fill. Because even if you end up working at Nyx's Kingdom, you would get to pick and choose your hours. And in your downtime, you can't have sex *all* the time."

Fighting a blush, Meadow wondered if she could start writing again. She'd loved creating stories as a teen, until her magic had appeared and upended her world.

As she thought about writing ideas down in her journal, Nora spoke up. "I'd love to read anything you write, once you get started, Meadow. Whilst I'm much better than I was before I met River, reading about a strong heroine might inspire me to try even harder to be one myself."

Meadow took one of Nora's hands and squeezed. She'd learned a little more about the female's past in recent days—about her being sold as a breeder by her father and being sexually assaulted, as well as her babies being taken from her—and couldn't help but say, "You're amazing already, Nora. We aren't all on the same journey, and we have to take the wins when and where we can."

Nora nodded. "I like that. And yes, we should. *All* of us."

Ack, she meant her, too. "I'm trying, but it's going to take more lessons and being able to control my magic in public without a training bracelet before I stop hating my powers."

"Trust me, I understand better than most that it takes time to change routines or how you see the world. If you ever want to talk, I'm here. I know I'm not your blood-sister, but I always wanted sisters growing up, and I'd love you to be mine, just like Yesenia has become one."

"Hm, a vampire sister. I'd like that, and not just because my father would have a heart attack if he knew about it, either. You've been so kind to me, Nora, and I really appreciate it. You're far too good for River."

Laughing, Nora shook her head before replying, "Not true, but thank you." She tilted her head and asked, "So, will you go to the ball at Nyx's Kingdom tonight? It's a masked affair, and we can even do your hair to hide your ears, if you like. But it might be nice to take a break from your lessons and have some fun. It'll also give you a chance to see Laurie and Joseph in their element. Well, more Laurie than Joseph, but both will dance, if you ask them to."

"Er, I don't know how to dance."

Nora tapped her chin. "I'm sure we have enough time to teach you how to waltz. If you're not too tired, that is?"

Before she could change her mind, she blurted, "No, I'm not too tired. I'd love to learn the waltz and go tonight."

Nora clapped her hands. "Brilliant. Then let's see what you have in your wardrobe and then I can teach you the waltz. We might even get River to help, as I've taught him, too."

Yesenia snorted. "I'd pay to see River dance."

Nora said, "He's quite good, actually. Even if he holds me a little too close."

Meadow imagined Joseph holding her close before giving her to Laurie, who definitely moved his hand too far south, and anticipation coursed through her.

While she had a long way to go before she could be considered a social butterfly, she didn't have to hide away any longer. And she'd always dreamed of balls and dancing and the things that rarely happened in the twenty-first century any longer.

Damn it, I'm tired of cowering. I want to have fun, and this will be like a dream.

Even so, she needed one caveat. "I can wear long gloves over my training bracelet, though, right? I don't want it to come off."

Yesenia nodded. "We'll make it work. They have loads of buttons on a lot of fancy gloves here, so we should be able to fit one over the bracelet easily." She studied Meadow for a beat and asked, "So that's a yes?"

"Yes, I'll go. Although I don't know what to wear."

Nora threaded her arm through Meadow's. "More of your dresses arrived today, including one I bought for you as a gift, just in case you ever wanted to attend a masquerade ball at Nyx's Kingdom."

Yesenia jumped in. "And I brought along some of the jewelry Leo inherited from his ancestors. You'll look like a queen when we're through!"

Meadow laughed. "This is like when I was really little and you liked to dress me up."

She'd seen some of the photos before their father had kicked Yesenia out and burned them all.

Yesenia winked. "This will be even better since you actually *want* to dress up. Now, let's go. There's a lot to do and not much time to do it."

And as her sister and sister-in-law taught her to dance and helped her dress, Meadow laughed and smiled, and all around had more fun than she'd had in a long time.

However, as much as she loved spending time with the two females, she was looking forward to the ball.

And by the time she was in the carriage and on her way, she tapped her foot and did her best to push aside the past, her worries, and anything negative. She wanted to have fun, get to know her two vampires, and maybe forget about the rest of the world for a short while, too.

Chapter Sixteen

Joseph stood at the edge of the ballroom and watched as patrons danced in the center of the floor.

Tonight was one of the tamer Nyx's Kingdom events, with clothing being required, but everyone was free to touch as much as they wanted, which meant many of the couples were kissing or caressing or dancing with their bodies close together.

The first time they'd had a tamer masquerade ball, Joseph had asked Laurie why. To him, it seemed the opposite of what their members paid for.

However, Laurie had explained that sometimes people wanted to pretend they were at a ball hosted by someone rich or powerful, but one where they could break the rules. So the ballroom had the appearance of being grand and proper, and yet the attendees were allowed to be slightly improper in public before being even more so in private.

The success of their first mostly proper masquerade ball had resulted in one every month, and attendance numbers had never dropped but rather increased, to the point there was usually a waiting list.

As Joseph glimpsed one couple who liked to frequent the ice and fire play room, he resisted a smile. To see them dressed to the nines, merely dancing and holding each other close, was such a contrast.

But as they twirled past him, he glimpsed the devotion in their eyes, and he longed for the same.

Oh, he had it from Laurie, and being able to give and receive the same looks with him since being blooded had helped. However, he longed to get the same from Meadow as well.

After the last time they'd seen her, when she'd been crying, Joseph had nearly risked going back into the fae witch's territory to check in on her. To ensure she hadn't cried again and was still progressing in her magic lessons.

And most especially to have her between his legs again, even if it were only to give her a massage.

It'd been so long since he'd had a female. He could easily waggle a finger and have his choice from inside the pleasure house, but none of them were quite right. Their hair was the wrong color, or their eyes, or their height.

Meadow was soft and beautiful and the perfect height, where her cheek would rest on his chest when he wrapped his arms around her.

A female shifter walked up to him, waved her fan, and smiled. "Will you ever dance with me, Joseph?"

He took her hand and kissed the back of her glove. “I’ve been blooded, Beth. If you ever want to find your fated one, you need to look elsewhere.”

She pouted. “We could still have some fun.”

One of the most difficult parts of his job was straddling the line between pleasing the patrons and standing his ground. “Alas, not with me. There are some new guests tonight, though—a few fae witches. One of the males has been staring at you all evening. He’s in the bright yellow waistcoat.”

She continued fanning herself as she discreetly spotted the tall fae witch with ginger hair. “Hm, it’s been a while since I had a ginger. Maybe his magic could make things interesting.”

With that, she turned and slowly made her way toward the male. Just as the pair headed to the dance floor, Joseph noticed a latecomer to the ball at the top of the grand staircase.

Despite her mask, he instantly recognized Meadow Vale.

She wore a dress in dark blue with a type of gauze that glinted under the lights. It hugged her upper body before billowing down to the floor. Her hair was also twisted and braided intricately, with some pearls placed throughout it.

As she descended and looked around, he headed toward the staircase. He reached it just as Meadow recognized him and hurried down the last few steps. She smiled shyly as he took her hand and kissed the back of her glove. “I’m so happy you came. You look beautiful.”

She touched her hair. "You don't think it's too much? Nora and Yesenia went a little overboard."

He guided her to the bottom of the stairs and threaded her arm through his, never breaking eye contact. "Not a bit. You blend in perfectly, and everyone will be asking me later who's the gorgeous female in blue."

Her look said she wasn't quite sure if he told the truth about that, even though vampires couldn't lie.

The latest dance song ended, and before she could doubt him, he blurted, "Would you like to dance the waltz with me?"

As soon as he said it, he mentally cursed. She probably didn't know how to waltz.

She beamed up at him. "I'd love to. Nora taught me, and it's been on my bucket list forever."

He gently guided her toward the floor as he asked, "What's a bucket list?"

"Oh, like a list of things you want to do before you die."

He took one of her hands in his and placed the other at her waist. The music started, and Joseph ensured Meadow was fine with the steps before asking, "And what else is on your list?"

"Oh, mostly dumb stuff. I'm sure you don't want to hear about it."

He pulled her a little closer. "I want to hear everything about you, love. I wouldn't ask otherwise."

She searched his gaze. "I'm not sure I really understand why, but I'll answer and give a few if you promise to do the same?"

He smiled. "Deal. And that might be one of your first introductions to a vampire's love of negotiating."

She laughed. "I've heard about it, of course, but neither Nora nor Leo has done it with me yet. You're my first."

He leaned down and whispered, "Laurie and I will introduce you to more intricate deals later."

Her heart rate kicked up, and he took a second to revel in her heat and scent.

What he wouldn't give to be able to take her to a back room, strip her, and kiss every inch of her body before tasting her sweet blood.

Focus, Joseph. Give her a good night out first.

Leaning back, he arched an eyebrow. "So, what's on your list?"

Meadow concentrated on the steps for a second before replying, "Mainly to travel and experience new foods. Oh, and to write a book."

"I haven't traveled much myself, but I would like to one day, especially to Italy or France."

"The food would be amazing in either country, as well as the wine. Although it's weird because there are various ruins and tours and things back in my time, and yet I don't know if they are here."

"There are a lot of ruins or old buildings, but few have strict rules for visiting. Some of the most popular destinations do it out of necessity, such as in Egypt, but not many of the smaller ones."

"If that's true, then there are probably a lot of stupid tourist deaths. You know, people who think it's a good idea to climb a crumbling structure and then fall off."

He smiled. "I am not that kind of person, so don't worry."

"I know. Even Laurie, who seems a bit more impulsive than you, isn't stupid."

"Everyone is more impulsive than me, in general." At her strange look, Joseph decided to change the subject back to Meadow. "But you mentioned writing a book. What would it be about?"

Her cheeks turned pink. "Um, you know, romance and adventure and kick-ass heroines who can stand alone but are stronger with their perfectly imperfect partner."

"Hm, like a pirate adventure full of naughty bits?"

She snorted. "Naughty bits? Really? Is that what you say here?"

"Nyx's Kingdom is the epitome of a naughty house, love."

She smiled and shook her head. "It's so...British. But I like to call those parts steamy bits, or sexy bits, and in my stories, it would be part of the emotional journey and not just for thrills. Because for me, sex is an important part of a relationship."

Meadow fell silent and stared at his necktie.

"Meadow, look at me, love." Once she did, he continued, "I know you've had some horrible experiences in the past, but you enjoyed what Laurie and I did with you before, right?"

She bobbed her head.

"Good. Because it's important for us as well. We've

had some, er, difficult situations where a female didn't fancy both of us, or didn't like the fact our attention was evenly divided between all partners instead of solely on her. Whereas with you, I don't think that's a problem. Am I right?"

Joseph waited for her answer, aware that it could dash his future dreams, but knew it was important to always hear the truth when it came to this.

MEADOW NEARLY TRIPPED over her own feet when Joseph steered the conversation to about her, Laurie, and Joseph and what they'd done in that secret room before.

And now? With Joseph holding her so close, she wished they could be like some of the other couples who'd discreetly left the room to probably do naughty things, as Joseph liked to say.

But then uncertainty had flashed in his eyes when bringing up being part of a threesome again. He must've been hurt deeply in the past to still be so hesitant about her wanting him as much as Laurie.

And she didn't like it.

She leaned closer, until her breasts brushed Joseph's upper abdomen, and she finally replied, "I told you, I love the stories where they all love each other. Having multiple guys centered solely on me, all the time, would probably be too much. But if the love is shared between three people, then it's probably more manageable. If that makes sense?"

"Those are stories, though. Now that you've had more time to think about it, how do you feel? Do you fancy one of us more than the other?"

Searching his gaze, she asked softly, "Who hurt you, Joseph? Because I'm almost certain someone did."

She expected him to shut down, change the topic, and ignore her question. No male, apart from her brother, had ever wanted to talk about his past or feelings. And yet, Joseph had shared about his parents. That had been horrific, for sure, but it wasn't the only scar he carried from his past.

He leaned down and murmured, "In our longest relationship, a female fancied Laurie and merely tolerated me. Barely, in fact. And it was difficult because Laurie falls in love quickly, and it blinded him to her faults. I should've said something, but I didn't want to hurt him. Especially since it was before our frozen state and I didn't know if our futures would be with us together or not."

As the music wound down and they stopped dancing, she raised a hand to trace Joseph's jaw. "I'm still getting to know you both, but I don't like one of you more than the other. I do want to know more about both of you, though. So much more."

He lowered his head, stopping just shy of her lips. "I'm glad," he murmured before kissing her.

Meadow barely noticed people moving around them as Joseph's tongue caressed her own, and his hand moved to cup her butt and he pressed her against him.

And she instantly felt his hard cock.

He wanted her.

Without her magic.

And it was one of the sexiest things in the world to her.

She stood on her tiptoes, kissing him back and trying to press even closer against him.

Eventually Joseph gentled their kiss and pulled back to murmur, "Keep kissing me like that, love, and we'll give everyone a free show. It won't bother me, but I don't think you're ready for that yet."

Her cheeks burned, but she never looked away from Joseph's brown eyes. "No. And, er, what about Laurie? Shouldn't he be with us, too?"

He caressed her cheek. "Most of the time, yes, we'll all be together. But sometimes, we aren't. Sometimes it'll be one-on-one, mixed between us. Is that okay?"

Reason returned to her mind, and she nodded. "That seems the most real way to handle a three-person relationship. I'm guessing you and Laurie have already hooked up since you were blooded."

He never stopped lightly stroking her cheek. "Yes. But it doesn't mean I want you any less. I'm greedy and want you both, in any and every way I can have you."

She smiled. "I want you both, too. And I think for the first time, it should be the three of us together. Do you think Laurie will be free anytime soon?"

He stilled. "You want to spend the night with us?"

For a beat, she hesitated as fears of what could go wrong coursed through her.

But then she pushed it back. She wanted this, more than anything. And if she couldn't give Laurie and

Joseph a chance, a real chance, to prove everything they'd promised, the past would win.

Her father would win.

And Meadow refused to let that happen.

"Yes, I want to spend the night with you both. Maybe not the full claiming yet since I've never had a vampire bite me before. But us all together and seeing where it leads? Yes, I want to try it."

He scooped her into his arms. "Laurie's overseeing a smaller event, but I can send an employee to fetch him."

"Can you both just drop everything and leave like that?"

"We've had years to train staff that we trust. So, yes."

She tightened her arms around his neck a bit, leaned up, and kissed him gently. "Then carry me off, Joseph. Before I change my mind."

He twirled with her, and Meadow laughed before he strode toward the double doors leading out of the room. She noticed quite a few smiles, but also a few glares, as they left. He even whispered to one of the staff, probably about Laurie, before exiting the ballroom.

Her heart thundered in her chest, and Joseph led her through a secret door and then a hallway before stopping at a room near what had to be the top floor of the building. Then he managed to turn the doorknob, enter, and she blinked. Because leaning against the doorjamb of a room to the side was Laurie.

He wore a formal suit as well, except his tie was undone and hanging from his neck.

His cocky grin made her stomach flip, in a good way.

Joseph snorted. "You made good time."

Laurie walked up to them. "I had a good reason." He turned Meadow's face toward him and kissed her.

His kiss was gentler, exploring her mouth, before he finally broke the kiss. "Hello, Miss Vale."

She smiled. "Hello, Laurence."

Laurie made a face. "Please don't use my full name."

"Then call me Meadow, or Em."

Laurie tilted his head. "Em?"

"Er, it was a childhood nickname, for the first letter of my name. But you don't have to use it, if you don't want to."

"Hmm, I think Emmy suits you better."

Meadow had sometimes wished for a different, more normal-sounding name since people had made fun of her so-called hippy name, joking about her parents being on drugs or something. When, in fact, her mother had loved nature—she'd been able to manipulate plants with her magic. And one of her favorite places in the world had been a little meadow close to her childhood home.

And because her mother had given it to her, she'd never wanted to change it fully.

But a special name, just for her, from her two males?

She rather liked that.

Meadow nodded. “Call me Emmy, then.”

“Our Emmy.” Laurie kissed her quickly. “Can we unwrap you now, pet?”

Self-consciousness flared, but as she looked between Laurie and Joseph, and their heated gazes, she willed herself to be stronger. To believe that they wanted her.

Wanted to see her naked, even if she wasn’t super thin.

After taking a deep breath, she nodded. “Yes, please. As long as I get to see you two naked as well.”

Without another word, Joseph carried her into a bedroom with an enormous bed, set her on the floor, and after both of the males kissed her gently, they began undoing the buttons on her dress and gloves.

And with each bit of skin they revealed, she grew hotter and wetter, and by the time she wore nothing but her training bracelet, she resisted covering her breasts or her privates.

Then Laurie and Joseph started shedding clothes, and she forgot about everything but their broad chests—noticing the smattering of hair on Joseph’s but how Laurie’s had none—and eventually her eyes moved down to their cocks.

Hard and long. Because of her.

Laurie murmured, “Get on the bed, Emmy, so we can worship every inch of your gorgeous body.”

Taking confidence from their gazes, she quickly crawled onto the bed and sat, crossing her arms over her belly.

The two vampires stalked over to her, and they each

took one of her hands. Joseph murmured, "Don't hide from us, love."

Laurie leaned down, kissed her lips and then each of her breasts before lingering on her belly. His hot breath danced across her skin as he said, "I've never wanted a female more in my life. Tell me I can make you come with my mouth."

She swallowed, his gravelly voice making her shiver, and she whispered. "Yes. Please."

He leaned back. "Then lie down for us, pet, so we can feast."

Meadow swore Laurie must have the power of persuasion, even if he was a vampire, because she did as he said without thinking and waited, hoping and wishing this could be as good as any of the scenes she'd read before.

Don't set your expectations too high. Never before has a male wanted to put his mouth there, *and you know it.*

But then Laurie and Joseph joined her on the bed, and as they touched her, she forgot about everything but the two vampires and how they made her hot and needy and desperate, more than she'd ever felt before in her life.

Chapter Seventeen

Laurie caressed Meadow's breasts, her belly, and then her thighs. "I can't believe how beautiful you are, and I can't wait to taste you, pet."

The blush on her cheeks deepened, and he resisted a smile. Someday, their female wouldn't bat an eyelash at their bed play.

But she wasn't there yet, and just the fact she wanted them both so soon, trusted them both so soon, meant the world to him.

And he wasn't about to fuck it up.

He continued to caress her thighs, never breaking eye contact, and eventually Meadow murmured, "You don't have to do it if you don't want to. I know no male has ever wanted to before."

He growled. "And those males were bloody stupid and selfish."

Joseph leaned down to nuzzle Meadow's cheek as

he said, "We both want to taste you, Emmy. I can help him, if you'll let me."

The image of Joseph's tongue battling his own to stroke Meadow's clit made his cock even harder.

She flushed even pinker. "Um, okay. I can try taking you with my mouth later, too."

Laurie rubbed slow circles on her inner thigh, wanting to ease her tense muscles. "Whilst I can't wait to feel your hot, wet mouth around my prick one day, this isn't a quid pro quo, pet. Bringing you pleasure will make me happy, make us both happy. Tonight will only go as far as you want it to."

She tucked a section of hair that had fallen out of its pins behind her adorable pointed ear. "As long as you're sure you still want me, even after seeing all of me, then I'm open to almost anything."

He moved until he was at her other side and leaned closer. "You're fucking perfect, Meadow Vale. Curves in all the right places, and tits I want to hold and suck and play with for days. Anyone who ever told you differently before didn't recognize the prize they had."

Joseph gently moved her head to look at him, and he said, "You're the most beautiful female I've ever seen. And remember, I can't lie. But know one thing, Emmy." He leaned closer to her face. "By the time you leave tonight, you will never again doubt how much we want you."

Her breathing had picked up, and Laurie noticed her racing pulse. His fangs ached to taste her sweet blood, but she'd asked them not to do that tonight, and he would honor her request.

Soon. Soon he'd be able to bite her neck and claim her properly. The only problem would be deciding whether he or Joseph would do it first.

Or maybe they could do it together.

Meadow's voice brought him back to the present. "Then hurry up and show me how much you want me."

Pushing her legs wide, Laurie lowered his body between them until his mouth was a scant few inches from her core. Despite her nervousness and doubts, she was already glistening.

The combination of her heat and scent made him lick his lips. "Time to begin."

He licked her slit slowly, reveling in her sweet honey on his tongue, and groaned. He noticed Joseph sucking one of Meadow's nipples, and he focused back on teasing and licking and lapping her core, driving her mad without ever quite touching her clit.

Between his mouth and Joseph's, Meadow was soon wriggling and arching toward them, and digging her fingers into the sheets.

One day, he'd take her to the edge, back off, and do it over and over again, until she begged.

Tonight, however, he wanted to show her what true pleasure felt like.

He reached out and touched Joseph's side, the signal for him to help.

As Laurie continued to tease her cunny, Joseph finally kissed his way down until he stopped just above Meadow's bundle of nerves.

Laurie ran his tongue upward and flicked the

bottom of her clit at the same time as Joseph caressed the top. Their tongues touched and battled as they increased their pace over Meadow's pleasure spot. She even put a hand on each of their heads, pushing them closer, and Laurie grunted, the signal for them to start the grand finale.

Which meant Laurie taking her sweet little clit into his mouth, suckling just long enough, and releasing. She cried out, but then Joseph did the same, and they alternated a few times before Meadow screamed in ecstasy. Laurie returned his tongue to her center, and gently fucked her as her orgasm went on and on, no doubt aided by Joseph's teasing of her clit.

Eventually she slumped onto the bed, and both he and Joseph gentled their movements. Once they both lifted their heads, Laurie kissed Joseph long and deep, their tongues caressing and absorbing both the taste of each other and Meadow on Laurie's tongue.

Once their kiss gentled and ended, they both kissed their way up Meadow's body, until they lay to either side of her. She raised her hands and put one to each of their jaws. "That was amazing. Truly, I never thought it could be like that without some vibrating toy."

Laurie smiled, kissed her for a few seconds, and then replied, "I'm more than happy to add toys later. But for now, you'll just have to settle for us."

Joseph kissed her and then said, "Tonight is for you, and we're at your command. We can hold each other and go to sleep, or do more. There is absolutely no pressure."

Meadow glanced between them, and Laurie struggled not to blurt out what he'd like to do to her next. But Joseph told the truth—this night was for Meadow. And unlike casual bed partners in the past, her wants and needs and feelings mattered to him. Mattered to him and Joseph both.

Not just because of the claiming or how gorgeous she was, either. She'd already found a way to help lift Joseph's moods by simply being herself. And if Laurie ever lowered his mask of the carefree male, she might even help him as well.

His past struggled to break free, but he pushed it aside. There would be no darkness in this bed tonight, no matter how much effort it took for him to stave it off.

Meadow was still floating on a cloud from her orgasm when they asked what she wanted to do next.

Part of her was greedy and wanted their mouths on her again.

And yet, they'd both made her come twice and never asked for anything in return.

The thought of them suffering yet again without complaint, to please her, made her determined to be bolder and ask for what she wanted. "I want us all together. I-I'm not sure I can handle both of you inside me at once, yet, though. But, er, I'm sure you can figure that out?"

The cock to each side of her hip turned even harder.

Laurie cupped her breast and toyed with her nipple, making it hard to concentrate as he said, "We can, pet." He hesitated before asking, "Who do you want inside you first?"

For a second, she saw doubt in Laurie's eyes. Maybe at some point he'd recognized the situation with Joseph and their former female, as well as the hurt it'd caused him.

"I don't care. You're both super sexy and great kissers. I, um, don't want a baby right now, though. But I'm guessing you have magical things to prevent that?"

Her heart warmed at the joy she saw in first Laurie's eyes and then Joseph's.

The two of them together was what she liked, what she wanted, and she couldn't imagine ignoring one instead of embracing them both.

Whoever that female had been, she'd been a fool.

Laurie nodded, and Joseph held up his hand and pointed as he said, "One ring is to prevent us being affected by magic, and the other is to keep us from impregnating anyone."

And since paranormals didn't have or pass on sexual diseases, it meant they could play without consequences.

Heat bloomed low in Meadow's belly. Despite her recent orgasm, she wanted more. "Good. And maybe you can both be briefly inside me before we get to the main event."

Laurie smiled. "Main event? Like for a circus?"

Meadow laughed. "No, no. Just, well, us all grunting and moaning and stuff at the end."

Joseph traced her cheek. "For someone who wants to write a book with naughty bits, you get embarrassed talking about it."

Her cheeks heated. "I'm much better at writing than talking."

Joseph kissed her. "I'm not teasing you, I promise. I find it adorable."

Laurie grunted. "What book with naughty bits? I feel as if I missed something."

Meadow shook her head. "I haven't written it yet. But I'll tell you more about it. After. If you make me… come again."

Heat flared in both males' eyes again.

Who'd have thought I could talk a little dirty?

Given her track record with males finishing before they'd barely started, it was a whole different experience with Laurie and Joseph. It was more than just sex and orgasms—she was having fun.

Laurie ran a finger through her slit, and she sucked in a breath. He chuckled and added, "Well, let's get started then because I want to hear about this naughty book of yours."

He shared a glance with Joseph before she felt Laurie's cock pushing inside her. She'd barely registered the fact before Joseph was kissing her as he massaged her breasts.

Then Laurie was fully inside her, and she moaned. Joseph took advantage, taking the kiss deeper and lightly pinching her nipples.

But after a few slow, deep thrusts, Laurie was gone. She cried out, but Joseph broke the kiss and moved between her thighs. "We're just getting started, love."

Then he pushed inside her pussy, so thick and hard, and she arched upward. Only a second later, Laurie took her mouth and ran his hand down her front, until he could lightly strum her clit.

He eventually broke the kiss and murmured, "Joseph will take you this first time. But just know that I'm dreaming of when I can feel your tight, hot cunny gripping my cock again, Emmy."

"I'll dream of it, too."

He grinned, kissed her once more, and then kissed down her body, flicking her clit a few times with his tongue, before kissing his way up Joseph's chest.

Joseph continued to thrust slowly as Laurie kissed him. Watching the two males make out with Joseph inside her made even more wetness rush between her thighs. There was so much passion between them, but it didn't seem like more or less than what they'd shared with her.

Could the three of them really make this work long-term?

Maybe forever?

Not wanting to wish for the impossible, she merely moved her hips to increase the friction. Laurie broke the kiss with Joseph, kissed his shoulder, and moved behind him.

Joseph took her breasts, fondled and gently squeezed them, before leaning over to kiss her too.

With him bent over, each thrust rubbed against her clit, and she moaned and arched up toward him.

Then Joseph moaned and lifted his head, bracing himself on the bed. Laurie was behind him, thrusting slowly, and his gaze met hers.

He continued moving, and soon Joseph started up again. Maybe if she'd been clear-headed, she would've admired the way they coordinated everything. But Joseph's thick cock moving inside her, and Laurie and Joseph's moans, and the way the bed started hitting the wall, consumed all of her attention.

Then Joseph pressed against her clit, and she screamed as wave after wave of ecstasy, even more intense than before, shot through her.

She barely heard the low, long groans from the two males as they stilled. Meadow was floating on a cloud of pure bliss, wondering if this was what taking drugs felt like.

Struggling to stay awake, she watched the two males cleaning her up and then each other before Laurie turned her onto her side and spooned her from behind. Joseph then curled against her front, putting his arms around them both.

She snuggled into them, their heat like an electric blanket, and she murmured, "That was definitely different from anything I've ever done before, but in a good way."

The males both chuckled. Joseph kissed her gently as Laurie nuzzled her neck and murmured, "There's still so much to show you, Emmy. We do, after all, run a pleasure house."

"True. I kind of want to see more of it, too." She hesitated and added, "But only if I can wear real clothing. I don't want to walk around half-naked."

Joseph moved a hand to her hip and stroked it. "Good, that means we're the only ones who get to see your lovely body in all its glory."

It was on the tip of her tongue to tell him to stop lying. And yet, their every touch and glance this evening had only conveyed desire and lust.

Try believing them. Maybe you were never with the right male before, one who wanted what you had to offer.

While Meadow didn't think she could just instantly dismiss her insecurities and be the bold, strong, don't-give-a-shit female she wanted to be, the first step was to let the past lie in the past and believe Laurie and Joseph.

She rubbed her ass against Laurie behind her at the same time she kissed Joseph.

Laurie groaned. "You're teasing us on purpose, aren't you?"

His cock was already hardening again. "Hmm, maybe." She ran a hand down Joseph's chest and touched his cock. As she stroked, she said, "Take me, Laurie, and I'll take care of Joseph this time."

And as Laurie entered her, Meadow stroked and caressed and played with tightening her grip, all while Joseph kissed her.

By the time all three of them had orgasmed, Meadow had forgotten all about her douche-y former lovers. And once they were all cleaned up again, she fell asleep in their arms, hoping they wouldn't hurt her.

Because if she wasn't careful, she could see herself falling for them.

Chapter Eighteen

The next morning, as light filtered through the curtains, Laurie held Meadow close and barely resisted waking her up to make love to her again.

Joseph had gone to get breakfast for them. Normally, they could just ring and ask for something to be brought up. However, two disgruntled patrons were refusing to leave even though the pleasure house had shut down a few hours ago. Since Joseph was better at handling that kind of situation, he'd gone, but not before murmuring something about giving Laurie some time alone with Meadow since he'd had her at the ball last night.

Part of him was thrilled to get to know their fae witch better. And yet, another part of him wanted to jump out of bed and find an excuse to leave. Not because he didn't want to spend time with her. But rather he was afraid that once she learned of how he'd failed his sister, then Meadow wouldn't want anything to do with him.

No matter how many times Joseph—or even Nora herself—had told him it would've been impossible for Laurie to have done anything differently, he still felt guilty.

Meadow stirred, her lovely, soft arse rubbing against him, and he pushed aside his memories to focus on what he hoped was his future. He kissed her neck. "Good morning, Emmy."

"Hmm."

"Not a morning person, are you?"

"I can be, although my work before was mostly at night. So I kind of became a night owl out of necessity. That works in your favor, though, since you're a vampire."

He hugged her a little tighter against his body. "Not just a vampire, but one who runs a den of sin that mostly functions at night. So you're a perfect fit."

Meadow rolled over until she faced him on her side. She placed a hand on his chest and lightly stroked it. His cock twitched, but he focused on her words as she asked, "I've been curious—how did you guys end up opening and running Nyx's Kingdom in the first place?"

He lazily played with one of her breasts, loving how her nipple beaded for him instantly. "It mainly started for selfish reasons. Not long after Joseph saved me from a street gang—one that had been intent on killing me to get my last remaining coins—I knew I wanted him. And after being together for a while, we were comfortable enough to admit that we both wanted a third bed partner to share. However, it was nearly impossible to find one since you can't just advertise it, and we didn't know enough trustworthy people to put the word out.

"However, Joseph had heard of a few human-run pleasure houses where they wouldn't bat an eyelash at multiple bed partners. However, almost all of them banned paranormals."

Meadow nodded. "Things seem more divided here than in my time. Not that it was perfect by any stretch, but we all kind of lived and mingled together, at least in the US."

"We're still a far cry from that in London, although my brother is working on changing that with the other Dark Lords."

"So back to your story—Joseph had heard about some pleasure houses. Then what happened?"

He traced her collarbone and up her neck as he replied, "Well, one night after a few drinks, I blurted out that we should open our own pleasure house for paranormals. I expected Joseph to laugh and say it was a stupid idea, but he didn't. No, instead he started to sketch out a business plan. I added the creative touches, and eventually, we had a solid idea. A few friends believed in us and gave us some funds in exchange for a percentage of the profits, and it didn't take long before word spread and we started doing well. Once Leo became the vampire Dark Lord, we could invite the fae witches and shifters. Then a few years ago, we started allowing some humans to join, too. And, well, our eventual goal is to expand even further by opening another establishment in the shifter territory. And maybe now that Leo's married to Yesenia, we can even have a place in the fae witch territory, too."

She searched his gaze. "And if you marry me, that gives you a higher chance of having one in the fae witch territory."

At the disappointment in her gaze, he cupped her cheek and said, "Don't ever bloody think that's the reason we want you, Meadow. You being yourself is enough. You've already helped Joseph, in ways I never could."

Curiosity sparked in her gaze. "And what about you, Laurie? You appear happy and teasing and charming, but I sometimes catch a glint of something else there. Something sad and painful. Won't you tell me why?"

As he caressed her cheek, his first impulse was to tease her or distract her with an orgasm. He'd always done that in the past with females who started asking him personal questions.

And yet, Meadow was different. She was genuinely curious, didn't seem to care much about his or Joseph's wealth, and instead wanted to know about him.

She might push you away, though. Do you want to risk it?

"Laurence." He frowned and scrunched his nose, but she continued before he could tell her not to use his full name again. "There, I got your attention. Why don't you like being called by your full name?"

Before he could talk himself out of it, he answered,

"My father always used it. He used all of our full names, and it brings back unpleasant memories."

Her eyes widened. "Oh, I'm so sorry, Laurie! I had no idea it was that serious. I never want to hurt you on purpose."

He stroked her cheek with a finger. "I know, pet. But you didn't know, so I can't be angry about it." He sighed and moved to rest his head on her shoulder. "My father was an absolute bastard. And not just because of what he did to my sister, but also because he convinced me that trying to help her would be a mistake." He wrapped his arms around Meadow. "I failed Nora completely, and she suffered because of it."

"I somehow think that's not the full truth."

"But it is. If I'd really cared about my sister, I would've moved heaven and earth to save her. And yet, at the first challenge, I ran away to live on the streets."

Silence descended, and Laurie waited for Meadow to shove him away and tell him never to touch her again.

But until then, he held her close, committing to memory how peaceful he felt in her presence.

MEADOW KNEW ONLY the basics of what Nora had been through, and she struggled to see how Laurie thought her suffering was his fault.

She needed more information. So as she stroked his back, she asked, "Why do you think you failed Nora? Given what I know of your father, he was a sick bastard. I mean, he basically sold his daughter out as a broodmare and didn't care what any of those males did to her. What could you have done to stop him?"

Laurie tightened his hold on her. "Something, anything. I tried once to sneak into the place they were holding her, but I got caught. My father beat me to within an inch of my life and said the next time he wouldn't stop. By that point, our father had sold Leo off as a soldier for twenty years, and I was all Nora had left here. I should've found another way. But no, instead I got scared and ran. Nora suffered several more years because of it."

She continued stroking his back and finally asked, "You're only two years older than Nora, right?"

"Yes, but that's not an excuse."

"Look at me, Laurie." Once his brown eyes met hers, her heart ached at the pain and guilt she saw there. She cupped his cheek and stroked her thumb against his skin. "What has Nora said about it all?"

He shook his head. "Nora's too kind and forgiving."

"So she said not to blame yourself?"

"Yes."

"Then she's right." He opened his mouth, but she beat him to it. "Your father was the vampire Dark Lord at the time, one who had no qualms about killing and abusing fae witches for the fun of it. If he nearly killed you once, then no doubt he would've followed through on his threat if you tried again. I'm sure you'll say that maybe it would've worked out, but maybe it wouldn't have. And then where would Nora have been once she entered her frozen state? Or, once your father died? She would've had one less brother to be there for her."

Laurie rolled away onto his back and ran his fingers through his hair. "They hurt her, Emmy. Badly. Not to mention they took away all of her babies. And maybe you're right that nothing I did could've helped her. But I should've at least tried to kill our father and end his cruel reign."

Meadow was silent for a second before she spoke up. "I can't begin to understand what it's like to take a life, but I imagine it would rest heavily on your soul, Laurie. And even if you had succeeded, could you have walked away without any consequences? By all accounts, your father had a small group of hardcore supporters, ones who would've sought revenge. Maybe not just with you, but Nora too. I don't claim to understand fate, but maybe it was meant to be this way. Your sister has become strong because of her past, just as it shaped you into who you are now."

Laurie lowered his hands and studied her for a few beats. Meadow wondered if she'd gone too far, but this was super important and not something she wanted to tiptoe around.

Besides, after all the hiding and half-truths she'd been forced to do to avoid her father, she was done trying to blend into the woodwork and go unnoticed. Done with holding her tongue out of fear.

Oh, it'd take time to say things without any hesitation. But she was determined to be more open.

Eventually, Laurie let out a breath and rolled onto his side. He propped his head on his hand and said, "I always thought that Nora said similar things just to smooth over the waters."

"Your sister is pretty wise, and incredibly happy now with River. She's living for the present and the future, and I think we should all learn from that."

He arched an eyebrow. "You too?"

She nodded. "I think you, me, and Joseph have all been hiding and running from our pasts, from things we wished to forget." She placed a hand on Laurie's warm chest again. "But maybe me starting your and Joseph's hearts was not only your new rebirth into life, but mine as well."

He moved closer and wrapped an arm around her. "I think some of the writer in you is coming out. And no, I'm not teasing you. It just makes me eager to read whatever you write."

She smiled. "You only want to read the naughty bits. But I promise you, they are integral to the story."

"Well, then you'll just have to hurry up and write it so I can read it and see for myself."

"I wish I could write a story with three main characters, but that might be too much for this time period."

He nuzzled her cheek, and Meadow leaned into the touch. He murmured, "Maybe eventually we can offer a special library here for patrons and see how they like the stories. Plus, Joseph will probably come up with a plan for how to get you published as well, even if the stories only have two main characters."

Meadow chuckled. "Well, I'll just have to ease the Victorian period in with steamy romance novels, and

I'll definitely have to use a pen name." Laurie tried to kiss her, but she leaned back and asked, "Before anything else, you need to tell me if you're going to try forgiving yourself for the past, Laurie."

He brushed some hair off her cheek. "Only if you also try putting the past behind you so you can embrace the female who emerged after starting our hearts."

"I'm going to try. But it's going to take some time to come to grips with it all, especially about my magic."

Laurie moved his hand to her training bracelet and touched it. "I believe in you, Emmy. You'll conquer and master your powers. And maybe helping Michael will show you how much good you can do with them."

"I hope so."

There was a knock, and Joseph entered, pushing a cart into the room. "Breakfast is served."

Meadow's stomach rumbled, and she was about to apologize when Laurie rolled out of bed, scooped her up, and carried her to a chair near the fireplace.

For a split second, she was embarrassed about sitting naked on his lap.

But then Joseph sat on the arm of the plush chair, and they both offered her tidbits. And by the end, they were all kissing and spent the rest of the morning in bed, having sex and laughing and all-around giving Meadow hope that these two males really could become her future here in the past.

Chapter Nineteen

Meadow spent the next week working on her magic lessons with Nadia during the day and spending most of the evenings with Laurie and Joseph at Nyx's Kingdom.

By now, she'd seen all the rooms inside their pleasure house, and had even mustered up the nerve to walk around one night with them, among all the people.

Seeing Laurie and Joseph in their element, in charge and competent and skilled in handling difficult members, only made her like the pair even more. Combined with them all being a little less aloof after sharing their pasts and troubles, and Meadow was falling hard.

It was still difficult to accept that they both wanted her so much, or even cared about her progress with her magic. And yet, they were always interested and never dismissed her.

But no matter how many affirmations she used or journal entries she made, her magic and fear around it was still a problem.

And tonight would be the true test of her progress.

Nadia had assured Meadow that she was ready to help the shifter and his fated one, especially if everyone else was clear of the building. In truth, Nadia believed Meadow could limit it to just the pair. But after what had happened with Giles Dawson the first time, she didn't want to risk it, at least not until she'd had more training.

As her carriage slowed and stopped at the back entrance of Nyx's Kingdom, Meadow's palms were sweaty and her heart raced.

But instead of a footman, Laurie and Joseph opened the door and helped her down, kissing her hello as they did so. Once they were inside the building, she blurted, "I'm sorry again for your lost business tonight."

Joseph raised an eyebrow. "And we told you to stop apologizing. We occasionally shut down for a private event, so our members expect it. Besides, helping Michael might give hope to those suffering from the same problem. Ones who've been too afraid to say anything before."

Laurie jumped in. "Obviously we didn't advertise what's happening here tonight, but word will spread slowly, I'm sure of it." He took one of her hands and kissed the back of it. "Is there anything we can do to help you now?"

Even a week ago, she never would've voiced her

desire. But now she nodded. "You both giving me a hug and holding me for a few minutes would ease my anxiety."

Joseph placed a hand on her lower back and gently pushed. "Of course. Let's head into your room for some privacy."

After he nodded at some of the top security people —those in charge also had infused items to block out magic—they walked upstairs to the room they'd designated as hers. Not that she'd used it yet, but they had always given her the option of sleeping alone, if she wanted.

And it was funny, but after so many years of being alone and never thinking she could sleep with someone else in the room, Meadow now had trouble sleeping without at least one of her two males.

Once they entered the bedroom decorated in light blue, Joseph pulled her close and wrapped his arms around her before Laurie did the same from behind. After closing her eyes, she focused on the heat and familiar presence of Laurie and Joseph, how they believed in her, and how she wanted to help their friend.

The longer they held her, the more she relaxed, until she reluctantly said, "I'm ready and should probably meet the pair now."

Laurie released her, and Joseph kissed her long and slow. Once he finished, Laurie turned her toward him and kissed her a bit more urgently. By the time he finished, her cheeks were hot, and she wished she had a little more time to relax. With them naked and on the bed.

Laurie grinned. "You can have that later, pet. I know you've been curious about finally taking us both at the same time, after all."

She lightly swatted his arm. "I told you we could've done that last night, but you wanted to wait. Something about motivation."

Laurie winked. "Exactly."

She glanced at Joseph, who was trying not to smile, and narrowed her eyes. "You always tell me not to encourage him, but you do it all the time. Honestly, I thought you were on my side last night."

Joseph shrugged. "We didn't want you too tired or sore today. So it wasn't exactly encouraging him so much as making the logical choice."

She reached out and patted his crotch. "We'll see how logical you are later."

Joseph's eyes turned heated as Laurie laughed before saying, "Well played, Emmy. Well played."

The vampires each took one of her hands and squeezed, a question in their eyes. Meadow straightened up a little taller. "I'm ready. Let's go meet Michael and his fated one, and then I'll decide how to handle it from there."

The shifters were waiting in a lavish room on the top floor, one mainly used for shifter and vampire claimings. The bed was large and tonight would be covered in gold and green sheets, per the couple's request. Apparently, all the furnishings in the room could be changed out—even the wall panels were removable—to suit any color scheme, mood, or theme.

Not for the first time, Meadow wondered if they'd use it for when she finally allowed Laurie and Joseph to claim her. She was nearly ready but still worried that they'd do it, say they didn't want her, and leave.

No, no negative thoughts. Emotions influence your magic, so just focus on the good in your life right now. There is plenty, for sure.

Meadow, Joseph, and Laurie stopped outside the dark double doors, and Joseph knocked. A male voice said to enter, and they did.

Two shifters stood inside. Michael leaned heavily on a cane and had a dusting of gray hair at his dark temples. The female—who was named Abigail—wasn't much younger, also with some gray in her light brown hair, and was nearly as tall as Michael. They held hands, and the female glanced up at the male shifter, her heart in her eyes.

But there was also a flicker of doubt and sadness. Almost as if she was afraid this wouldn't work, and all was lost.

In that second, Meadow vowed to do whatever she could to help them. Because if she didn't, Michael and Abigail would both eventually lose their minds, be unable to control their inner animals, and maybe even be put down. And they didn't deserve that, especially when they both so clearly loved each other.

Michael bowed his head. "Miss Vale, I presume."

She smiled at him. "Yes. And you must be

Michael." She moved her gaze to the female. "And Abigail."

The female shifter smiled at her, the worry easing a little from her blue eyes. "Thank you so much for coming tonight, Miss Vale. I know fae witch Wielders are much sought-after and very busy."

And extremely expensive, was left unsaid.

Maybe Meadow should reserve a few spots a month for those who truly needed her services, regardless if they could pay. It wasn't the mercenary fae witch way, but she didn't care.

You need tonight to be a success first, so don't screw it up.

She replied, "Anyone my brother recommends is someone I want to help. But I'm sure you two have waited long enough, so let me explain how this will go, okay?" Once they nodded, she continued, "I'll sit behind that folding screen over there. Since my secondary power is persuasion, I'd prefer not to say anything so that your actions are all your own. I will merely weave lust and desire over Michael, and Abigail if needed, and if it is indeed a mental block, my magic will override it. I can't guarantee success, but I will do everything I can, I promise. And if there are still difficulties, I can even try speaking. But I want to leave that as a last resort since your claiming should be between you two."

Michael tightened his grip on Abigail's hand. "Please do whatever you can, Miss Vale. My Abby deserves her claiming more than anything."

Abigail added softly, "So do you, Michael."

He looked down at Abigail and kissed her. "I love you."

"I love you too."

For a split second, Meadow felt like a third wheel. Her past gigs had been mostly about steamy sex and longer stamina. Yes, most of her former clients had been in love, but there was something about Michael and Abigail that touched her more than anyone in the past.

She looked at Laurie and then Joseph as she said, "Will you two leave us?"

Joseph leaned over to whisper, "If you need us, we're just on the other side of the door."

Then Laurie whispered in her other ear, "We'll be cheering for you, pet. You're going to be brilliant."

Once they nodded farewell and left, Meadow said, "Let me know when you're ready for me to begin."

With that, she moved to sit behind the folded screen. The room was silent, and soon she heard the rustle of clothing and even some kisses. Then there was a creak on the bed, and Michael's voice reached her ears. "We're ready, Miss Vale."

"Let me gather my magic, and I'll begin."

Carefully removing her training bracelet, she placed it into her skirt pocket. Then she closed her eyes and concentrated on pulling magic from her fingertips, her toes, and even the top of her head into her body, slowly gathering it into the center of her chest. Bit by bit it grew, until the swirling red energy nearly consumed her entire body.

Taking a deep inhalation, she reached out and

found Michael's body and began weaving a net over him. Line by line, denser and denser, until she heard a gasp. Meadow ignored everything but keeping her net constructed and allowing her magic to drip from it onto Michael, until it was nearly a downpour.

Soon she heard moans and gasps and the usual sounds of sex. Smiling, Meadow continued keeping her magic over Michael, knowing he needed to bite Abigail as he came to fully mark her. Only then would his inner animal, as well as Abigail's, settle and be content.

A female screamed in pleasure, followed quickly by a low groan, and then there was merely heavy breathing.

Meadow began deconstructing her net and pulling back her magic. When she was finally done, she sat and waited, not wanting to interrupt what she thought was a happy moment.

After what seemed like half an hour of murmurs, and laughter, and sighs, Michael finally spoke up. "Thank you, Miss Vale. From the bottom of my heart, thank you. I have my Abby, and she's even agreed to be my wife. We'll thank you properly later, I promise."

"Of course. I'll take the side exit and leave you two alone. Come find me whenever you're ready."

Standing, Meadow went to the secret panel right next to the folding screen, found the latch as Laurie and Joseph had shown her, and exited into the main hallway.

As soon as she did, Laurie and Joseph rushed up to her, and she blurted, "I think it worked."

Laurie picked her up and swung her around before

kissing her. Joseph then took her face between his hands and kissed her as well. Joseph asked, "And how are you, love? Are you okay?"

She smiled as she fought back happy tears. "I-I helped them with my magic. Truly helped them."

Laurie took one of her hands and squeezed it. "Yes, you did. You helped two shifters claim each other and avoid madness. Michael regained something he'd lost, all because of you."

A tear trailed down her cheek, and Joseph wiped it away as she said, "Thank you, both of you. I-I never would've thought I could do something so meaningful for another. My father tainted how I thought about my powers. But now? There must be others who need help, but I also wonder if I can be creative for some of your members here. Maybe someday it'll become fun for me to use my magic."

Joseph tilted his head. "If you ever want to offer your services here, you are more than welcome. You'll set your own rules and rates, and I'm sure people will pay them."

"I'm not sure that I'm ready for that yet. However, I *am* curious about what I can do. With more training, both for my lust and desire powers as well as my persuasion one, I'm sure I could help Laurie with some of the event planning. I'd also bring in some money too, to help the business."

As soon as she finished speaking, Meadow regretted it. She was assuming they wanted a future with her, forever, and they might not.

Then Joseph and Laurie went to either side of her,

put an arm around her back, and then placed their foreheads to either side of her temple. Laurie spoke up. "That sounds like a perfect plan."

Joseph added, "But we'll go at your pace, Emmy. Whenever you're ready and want to try using your magic at Nyx's Kingdom, then merely say the word and we'll try."

She took a hand of theirs each. "Maybe I'll have some test events first, to be doubly sure I can contain it. I think I can, as I don't think I affected Abigail just now. But I want to be sure."

They both kissed a cheek and then Joseph said, "We'll figure it out. For now, we have to wait for Michael and Abigail to exit and meet with you. But after that?" His hand moved to her ass and squeezed. "I think you deserve some fun yourself."

She giggled just as Laurie squeezed her breast. "Maybe we have enough time right now…"

Meadow lightly swatted his chest. "I'm not going to greet my first clients in this time period in a bathrobe and mussed hair. You two can wait a little while longer." Laurie fake-pouted, and Meadow laughed. "Where are the two cool, confident businessmen I've seen every night so far? Surely you can put that mask on for a little while longer. Come on, let's go to the visitor's parlor and set things up for Michael and Abigail."

Laurie whispered, "If we go beneath your skirts, your hair won't get mussed."

She looked at Joseph. "Why aren't you backing me up on waiting and being patient, Joseph?"

He grunted. "I'm torn, actually. Because you are so beautiful when you're happy, and I only want to make you happier."

Meadow fell a little more for her vampires.

But she mustered up the confidence to herd them into the parlor, and they discussed a limited event she could run after the fae witch Autumn Festival.

And all the while, she never even noticed that she hadn't put her training bracelet back on.

Chapter Twenty

Several weeks passed, and Laurie had never been happier in his life.

He'd thought previous females had fit with him and Joseph, but those all paled in comparison to Meadow. She cared for them both, never favored one over the other, and screamed just as loud when she came regardless if it was he or Joseph inside her. She was the loudest, though, when they both took her.

The only thing he wished he could have was the claiming. However, Meadow still hadn't brought it up, and while the need to have her increased by the day, he was nowhere near madness levels. Plus, she'd been focusing on her magic lessons and even had a small event at Nyx's Kingdom coming up. Joseph said once she was more confident about her powers, she might be ready.

The hard part was keeping his feelings from their

fae witch because Laurie had fallen for her the day she'd helped Michael and Abigail. And his love had only grown as she became more and more confident, rarely wearing her training bracelet any longer, and all-around blossoming into the female she had always meant to become.

Joseph felt the same way about Meadow, but they'd agreed to wait to share their feelings until the claiming. The last thing they wanted was for her to feel pressured; it needed to be her decision and hers alone.

At least tonight was the fae witch Autumn Festival, and in a matter of hours, he and Joseph could show off Meadow and merely have a good time.

Right now, however, Laurie climbed the stairs of his brother's residence. Leo had sent a note for Laurie and Joseph to come, but Joseph had needed to tie up a few things at the pleasure house, so Laurie was here alone.

Leo summoning him was never a good thing, but Laurie hadn't done anything to merit a scolding, so his curiosity was piqued.

He reached his brother's office and knocked. Once Leo said to enter, he strolled inside and sat in the chair in front of Leo's desk. "I have arrived."

Leo arched an eyebrow. "Do you need a fanfare? Trumpets, perhaps?"

Laurie snorted. "Yesenia has definitely been good for you."

His older brother smiled. "She has." He sobered. "But let me get to the point—I received some information that might make you change your mind about attending the fae witch festival tonight."

He frowned. "What? Why? I thought our attending was part of your big plan to get closer to the fae witches."

"It is, but you should have all the facts before deciding if you should go with Meadow and Joseph."

While Leo was twelve years older than him and they'd rarely interacted as children, they'd grown closer after their father's death. And he knew his brother well enough now to understand that Leo was truly worried about something. "What is it, Leo? Just tell me."

Leo sighed and leaned back in his chair. "Well, Everett Black's people recently confronted and then killed a shifter traitor working with the French vampires. They'd hired him to betray his kind, and he wasn't the only one. That's about all they got out of him before he died."

Laurie leaned forward. "What? The French are hiring people to turn against their own kind?"

His brother tugged down his waistcoat. "Unfortunately, yes. However, that's not all—the amount they paid the shifter was exorbitant. Given how the vampires in France were mostly impoverished after the Napoleonic Wars, that means they either have a rich patron, or the rumor about the French vampires stealing jewels and riches from the humans executed during the 1780s Revolution is true."

"Bloody hell. Either way, large sums of money could tempt a lot of people and could become a massive problem."

"I agree, and I already have guards discreetly watching the few remaining supporters of our father;

they'd jump at the chance to take me down. Khan and Black are also trying to determine who might become a turncoat with the right incentive."

"Hence why you're warning me about avoiding the fae witch festival."

"Yes. Khan has tightened security and summoned his most powerful protection Wielders to place magical barriers and trigger traps around his territory. As a vampire, I have my doubts about protection magic. However, Yesenia convinced me we should still go, even if only briefly, to show I'm serious about improving relations between our two peoples."

Since Laurie and Joseph had hired some protection Wielders in the past to secure Nyx's Kingdom, he knew how effective they could be. Trigger traps, in particular, were great at freezing in place anyone who didn't meet the magic trap's requirements. A few could get past them, but it required strong magic and a very specific power. Namely, the power of disarmament. And to his knowledge, only two fae witches had that power in the UK.

He replied, "I doubt Khan would overlook anything, and so far I still feel confident about attending with Joseph and Meadow. The more relaxed and normal we appear, the more time we probably have to root out the traitors. We just need to be on our guard."

"That's not all, though. The shifter traitor revealed all the London shifter security protocols and secrets he knew to the French vampires. So not only might your security protocols be compromised since Nyx's Kingdom also caters to shifters, but Black is asking for help with his sister, Grace."

Everett Black was in charge of the shifters in the UK. And while Laurie had briefly met his younger sister once—a pretty but blind female who hadn't said much—he didn't know her well. Regardless, someone selling out their leader's family, especially a vulnerable one, was one of the lowest things a shifter could do.

Laurie replied, "Damn. I'll talk with Joseph, and if there's anything we can do to help Grace Black, just say the word. After what happened to Nora, I won't allow any male to take advantage of a female, if I can help it."

Leo nodded. "I've offered the same. Although, as hard as it is to admit this, Khan can probably protect her better for now. His residence and massive gardens are one of the most magically protected areas in the country, if not in Europe. It'll take time to prepare for her arrival, though, so Everett won't be attending the festival tonight. Instead, he'll be watching over her in a temporary location, guarded by some of the fiercest magic wielders who are loyal to Khan."

Tapping the arm of the chair, Laurie said, "With all of this going on, then why is Khan allowing the festival to happen at all?"

"Khan doesn't want to cause mass panic. And with the protection wards, only those who are invited can cross the magical barriers. There may be a few traitors amongst the fae witches, but between Khan's extra security and the ones I've offered as well, the chance of anything major happening is low."

"But won't that many vampires in their territory cause more problems than it solves?"

"Because of the wards and protection spells, it shouldn't be too bad. Me being there with Yesenia, as well as River with Nora, will help. Whether you bring Meadow or not is up to you, but I thought you deserved to have all the facts."

His first instinct was to say no and cancel.

And yet, fae witch protection wards were highly sought after and rarely used outside the fae witch territory—a few trigger traps alone had cost Laurie and Joseph a small fortune.

Plus, Meadow had grown leaps and bounds when it came to controlling her magic. If anything, she would probably be the safest among the three of them, especially with her secondary power of persuasion. He would leave the decision up to her.

However, an idea sparked about how his brother might turn this all to his advantage. "I'll talk with Meadow and Joseph. However, if you and Yesenia are going, then you should lay a trap here at the Fated Wheel to maybe catch some traitors."

Leo tilted his head. "What do you have in mind?"

The fact that his brother would even listen to him made Laurie sit up straighter. "Well, you could send nearly all of your guards from the gaming hell and make it appear an easy target. Keep some of the best ones hidden, wait to see if anyone breaks in, and if your most-trusted guards can capture one or more of them, we can get some information as well. Things that might help make the vampire territory safer."

"Hm, it's risky, but could work. Especially if Charlotte and John attend the festival too, then it would appear at least some of my top trusted employees were absent, making this place an irresistible target."

John and Charlotte Sakamoto were siblings who'd worked for Leo for a long time. John was the second-in-command, and Charlotte was in charge of the books. "It wouldn't seem suspicious, either, since Charlotte's partner is half fae witch."

Leo nodded. "True. Diana visits the fae witch territory at least once a month." He paused to stare at Laurie before adding, "Whilst I've always known you're cleverer than you let on, I wish you would've shown it more often, at least to me."

He shrugged. "It's better to appear the slightly foolish charmer and have people underestimate me." He hesitated before adding, "And I never knew if you'd ever take my suggestions seriously."

Leo leaned forward and propped his elbows on the desk. "I'm sorry you felt that way, Laurie. I was so consumed with making things better after Father's death that I shut a lot of people out. Yesenia helped me realize that, and I'm trying to do better. Promise me that if you have a suggestion, you'll share it? I can't guarantee I'll use everything, but it's always good to hear differing opinions."

Laurie whistled. "Yesenia deserves a jewel-encrusted crown for all she's done to help you."

Leo gave him a double-finger salute. "Sod off."

Laurie laughed, and then Leo's lips twitched before he said, "Meadow's helped you, too. Joseph did as well, but I think Meadow was the missing bit you needed, that you both needed. I think I even saw Joseph laugh the other day."

"She's bloody amazing, Leo. Meadow's so understanding and kind and loving, all whilst not letting me get away with everything."

"Good. Hopefully, you and Joseph marry her someday and keep her around forever."

"I'm working on it, but I won't pressure her."

Leo nodded. "Well, if River can win over Nora, then your chances are pretty good." Leo leaned back again and tapped a finger on the desk. "If you go to the festival tonight, then let me know and just be careful. If you see or hear anything, anything at all, tell me straight away."

Laurie nodded and stood. "I will. Thanks, brother."

"Anytime, Laurie. Now, fuck off. I have a lot to do and not much time to do it."

"Ah, and there's the old Leo I know." Leo opened his mouth, but Laurie beat him to it. "As long as Meadows says okay, we'll be going. I'm sure the females all have plans about where to meet and all the rest, so I'll see you tonight."

After saying goodbye, Laurie exited Leo's office and headed toward the back entrance to his waiting horse. As he rode home, he worried about leaving the safety of Nyx's Kingdom. However, when he put the question to Meadow, she said she wanted to go. After all, she'd dealt with unpleasant people before and didn't want to hide again. And so he and Joseph planned some extra security of their own, wanting to give their fae witch the night she dreamed of, and then got ready for the big event.

Chapter Twenty-One

Joseph didn't like drawing attention to himself. He'd always been as invisible as possible when living on the streets, not wanting the people who'd killed his parents to find him.

And later, when he'd had to interact with more humans at Nyx's Kingdom, it had been to avoid their prejudices because of his skin color.

Humans were less tolerant, and Joseph was used to that. However, whenever Laurie heard something disparaging about Joseph, he didn't hold back and usually beat the person senseless.

Which had been bad for business.

Over the years, Joseph had learned to be on the fringes and eject the worst offenders more discreetly. He got upset, of course. But to risk his freedom, his business, and anything else over a human's small mind wasn't worth it.

Besides, given the web of contacts and favors

Joseph had amassed over the decades, he could make their lives miserable from the shadows.

Still, he felt uncomfortable doing anything that made him stand out. So tonight, when Laurie had insisted they both paint designs on their faces and wear crowns for the festival, he'd fought it at first. However, as Laurie currently adjusted Joseph's crown and then stood back to admire his handiwork, Joseph merely arched an eyebrow. "Well?"

Laurie had opted for a silver crown and blue face paint. The design was intricate around his eyes—he'd used a mirror and done it himself—and stopped at his mid-cheek. It made his eyes stand out, and for a split second, Joseph wondered how Laurie would look with paint on his chest, too.

However, before his fantasy went too far, Laurie spoke again. "You look regal, handsome, and I wish that paint was edible so I could lick it off."

"Well, then, devise an edible one and we'll try it next time."

Laurie's eyes turned heated a second before he shook his head. "Remind me later. Maybe you can lick it off me as I lick it off Meadow, and she eats it off you."

Images of the three of them tangled in bed, tasting and touching and fucking, flashed into his mind. "Behave, Laurie. The last thing we need is to walk around with erections amongst the fae witches and have them think we're there to take whoever we want."

The lightness in Laurie's eyes died. "Like my father did."

"You would never do that, though. I hope you know that."

"I do. Still, it'll always be there between the vampires and fae witches."

Laurie's father hadn't shied away from using rape and torture in the war he'd started against the fae witches, back when Laurie had been a toddler.

Joseph walked over and took Laurie's shoulders, not wanting to smear the paint on his face. "Between us, Leo, Nora, and even the half vampire Stone Riley, we're trying to change that. We all have fae witch fated ones, and with time, that should become more common. I think one day we might even have open borders between all the territories in the East End."

"I might've scoffed at that before, but I'm a little more hopeful these days given all that Leo is doing to forge a closer alliance. Let's hope that future comes to pass."

Joseph kissed him gently before replying, "Tonight will help with that goal, I think. Speaking of which, if we don't leave now, we'll be late picking up Meadow. And I don't know about you, but I want to watch her walk down the staircase and admire her."

"Too bad it'll be in front of an audience," Laurie grumbled. "I'd rather see her in private and give her a proper hello."

"As much as I'd love to ravish her, too, we all need tonight, I think, to relax and try to enjoy the evening. Plus, we can spoil her in public, learn more about what she likes, and then use that knowledge to further win her outside of the bedroom."

Laurie laughed. "Always the strategist, aren't you?"

"If it gets me what I want, then of course."

He winked, and Laurie chuckled again before saying, "Between your heart beating again, being able to have sex again, and whatever magic Meadow has used on you—figuratively—some of the old Joseph has returned. I missed him, you know." He gently gripped the back of Joseph's neck. "I hope he stays around."

"It was mainly to protect myself, as you well know. But now? I don't have to protect my heart from you, or anyone else." Laurie leaned in to kiss him, but Joseph shook his head. "We'll be late. And if we ever want Meadow to pick us as her forever, we need to treat her with the respect she deserves."

"Normally I'm a gentleman, too. But having your handsome self in my life again, truly in my life, has addled my brains a bit. However, you're right—Meadow needs us more right now. And I can't wait to see what she's wearing for her costume."

Soon they were both sitting inside their carriage, discussing what to see and do that evening. In less than twenty minutes, they stood inside River and Nora's house, at the bottom of the stairs with the fae witch male. Leo was also there, and all four of them waited for the females to descend the stairs.

Leo tugged his waistcoat down before checking his pocket watch. "Maybe we should go check on them. Khan wants us there by eight, and it's already a quarter to."

River crossed his arms over his chest and shook his head. "You and your punctuality. A few extra minutes won't hurt. It took me long enough to do this." He waved to the paint on his face—a much simpler pattern in purple—and continued, "So I can only imagine how long it takes when they have to do their hair, too."

The fae witch male was still growing out his hair after arriving in the past with a shaved head. However, it barely reached his shoulders, and he wore it loose.

Leo rolled his eyes. "I can't believe I allowed Yesenia to talk me into painting my face too."

Laurie snorted. "Two lines on each cheek is hardly painting your face."

Joseph bit back a smile. Leo had two black streaks on either side of his face. He then added, "You could've picked a less menacing color."

Leo grunted. "It's not red, which is the only color Yesenia forbade me to use."

River sighed. "Let's not go around painting fake blood on our faces. These are fae witches, after all, not vampires."

Laurie jumped in. "Maybe we should have a vampire celebration, and then everyone can use red paint."

"That would be a bit macabre," Joseph stated.

Laurie shrugged one shoulder and pointed at himself. "Vampire. We have a reputation to uphold."

Joseph rolled his eyes, but before he could reply, movement at the top of the stairs garnered his attention.

Yesenia, Nora, and Meadow descended the stairs in a row—their outfits for the night were more flowing, like fae witch dresses of old—but Joseph's attention was fixated solely on Meadow.

She wore a dark blue dress. The sleeves were wisps of fabric that went to about her elbows, and the bodice hugged her breasts before loosely draping down her lush body, also with a multitude of fabric strips. Her face paint was gold, as were the decorations woven through her hair. Since her hair was pulled back, her pointed ears were on full display, made more noticeable by the cuffs of gold around the sides.

The latter were gifts from him and Laurie, and seeing her wearing them sent a rush of satisfaction and desire through him.

She kept her eyes downcast, though, and Joseph wanted to rush up the stairs, lift her chin, and tell her how bloody beautiful she was before kissing her senseless.

Then she finally met his gaze, and her eyes widened. Good. She'd seen how much he wanted her, and hopefully how gorgeous she was to him.

Her eyes moved to Laurie, and her cheeks turned even pinker. Joseph should look at Laurie's face to judge his reaction, but he couldn't tear his eyes from Meadow. The little wisps of fabric bounced and fluttered, drawing attention to her breasts. Ones he wouldn't mind taking out and sucking, until she moaned and begged for more.

Stop it, Joseph. No erections tonight, remember? Scaring the fae witches would be a bad thing.

When the three females finally reached the bottom of the staircase, each of the males went to their respective partner. Joseph managed to speak before Laurie did. "You're going to be the most beautiful female there tonight, love."

She replied, "You don't have to flatter me."

"It's not flattery. You're stunning."

Laurie jumped in. "He's right. I want you to eventually sit for a portrait wearing exactly this costume. You're like something out of a fantasy, pet."

She glanced between them before finally murmuring, "Thank you. And you both aren't too shabby yourselves."

Laurie stood taller. "Do we look like fae witch princes?"

She laughed. "I'm not sure what one looks like, but you're definitely two sexy princes. Or, maybe kings is the better term since the word prince is too childish for either of you."

Joseph smiled, took her hand, and kissed the back of it. "Then you are our queen tonight."

Laurie took her other hand, kissed it, and added, "Whatever you wish, we'll grant it."

Judging by the flash of heat in Meadow's eyes, she hadn't missed Laurie's invitation. Joseph was about to whisper something to turn her cheeks fully red when River cleared his throat. Loudly. "If you're done drooling over my sister, can we go?"

He and Laurie each turned and threaded one of Meadow's arms through each of theirs. Laurie spoke up. "We had to stomach you fawning over Nora, so you can handle our wooing of Meadow."

Nora smiled. "I, for one, am happy to see you fawn over Meadow, and she over you two."

River grumbled, but a look from Nora quieted him.

Leo took out his pocket watch again. "We need to leave. I don't want to be late for my first public appearance in the fae witch territory. I've met Khan in private, but I don't want the fae witches' first impression of me to be tardiness."

Yesenia leaned against him a little. "Yes, okay, Leo. Our carriage is out front, so let's go."

They all exited River's house, and Joseph surveyed the outside, instantly spotting the discreet guards they'd brought along. Only because he knew to look for them could he see them in the shadows.

Once inside the carriage, with Meadow sitting on one bench and Laurie and Joseph on the other, she finally spoke up. "I know you're both worried, but let's try to have fun tonight, okay? Being in a large crowd will be hard enough for me as it is."

Joseph leaned over and took her hand. "I'm sorry, Emmy. Rationally, I know trigger traps and protection wards are extremely powerful. And yet, this is my first time publicly out and about in the fae witch territory. Unlike in my home territory, I don't know all the nooks and crannies people could use to hide in and attack us."

She squeezed his hand in hers. "River took me on a tour of the area before they set up the stalls, stage, and dance floor. It's an open space, with the stalls mostly sitting in front of the shop fronts and homes. Since most of the homes are terraced, there isn't much space between them. Plus, I can protect us all, if it comes to it. I've used my magic to save myself before, and I can do it again."

Seeing her so much more confident made Joseph's heart warm. "Then I'll try my best to enjoy the night."

She beamed at him, and Joseph itched to haul her into his lap.

Laurie spoke up. "I tried telling him the same, and he wouldn't listen. It's nice having two against one now. I might win a few more debates this way."

Meadow shook her head. "Let's not keep a tally. By all accounts, vampires are far more competitive than fae witches, and I don't want to be stuck in the middle."

Laurie took her other hand. "Never, love. I'd never do that. But I will always tease you and occasionally irritate Joseph just because." He winked at Joseph. "He's fun to make up with, and I can't wait until we all get to experience that together."

And just like that, Joseph laughed. "How you go from making me want to glare at you to wanting to kiss you, I'll never understand, Laurie."

He waggled his eyebrows. "Just a talent of mine." He yanked Meadow's arm until she sat between them, perched on a leg each. "Now, kiss us, Meadow. We need to get it out of our system before we arrive and need to behave in public."

Joseph snorted, but as Laurie kissed Meadow, he ran a hand up under her skirts and found her wet and swollen already. She cried out as he stroked her clit, and she came within a minute. Laurie released her, and Joseph swallowed her cries as he continued to draw out her orgasm. After breaking the kiss, he held out his finger to Laurie, who licked it clean.

Meadow's voice was breathy as she said, "Well, that's a new record."

Joseph smiled. "We just need to dress up for you more often, I think."

She laughed. "You two are rather handsome tonight."

The carriage slowed, and Meadow squeaked. "Please tell me you have a handkerchief so I can clean up."

Laurie produced one and batted her hand away as he wiped between her thighs. Afterward, he sighed as he tucked it into a hidden compartment in the carriage. "I'd take it with me, but then I'd be hard all night."

Meadow lightly swatted him as she got up and sat back down on the opposite side. "Try to behave, Laurie. I know that's a big ask, but I want to make a good impression on these people."

Joseph sensed there was more to her words, maybe about the uncertainty of her future, but the carriage stopped and one of the footman-slash-guards knocked on the door.

Right then and there, he decided to talk with Laurie about giving her a memorable night in the not-so-distant future. One where they could prove to her she wasn't a temporary toy but the female they wanted to spend the rest of their lives with.

But for the moment, Joseph nodded at Laurie and opened the carriage door. It was time to prove to the fae witches that not all vampires were like Laurie's father, and that they were worthy of being Meadow's future husbands.

Chapter Twenty-Two

The night air helped to cool Meadow down after the little escapade in the carriage. She should've scolded Laurie and Joseph for what they'd done, but she hadn't been able to. They brought out a side of herself that she'd never realized existed—she liked being adventurous. Only with Laurie and Joseph, but still. It was fun and exciting, and she wondered what else they could encourage her to do.

Before she could dwell on how they hadn't said they loved her or wanted her as their wife, they reached the festival area and her mouth dropped open.

Magical lights hung from cords that created a spiral shape over the open green square. Under the multicolored lights was a temporary dance floor. Off to the side was a stage currently filled with musicians playing alongside instruments infused with magic to play on their own.

There were also small stalls lining the square, with

everything from food to clothing to small trinket souvenirs. There were also stalls displaying their services, complete with examples of what their magical powers could do—miniature trees grown into shapes, animals who had multi-color coats that sparkled, and even a station where a fae witch female was shaping and changing hair color with magic alone.

It was such an open display of pride and fun and magic that Meadow had never seen before. Yes, there had been some festivals back in the US, but her father had never allowed them to go. Then she'd gone into hiding, and most definitely hadn't been able to attend any.

Joseph murmured, "The sketches and articles I've read about the fae witch festivals didn't do them justice."

She smiled and looked up at him. "Hey, I'm a fae witch and even I'm impressed."

A familiar, cool voice came from behind her. "I'm glad you like it, Miss Vale."

She jumped and turned to find Dark Lord Khan a few feet away, near Leo and Yesenia.

For a second, she swore he looked uncomfortable with the crowd, but she had to be imagining it. Fae witches in this time period didn't tolerate leaders ruling from afar, like in the future, and so he had to be used to the attention.

Meadow finally found her voice. "It's beautiful, Dark Lord Khan. I'm glad we could come."

He inclined his head. "Apart from my own residence, this is the safest space within my territory right now. Please enjoy the night. If you need anything, there are security guards stationed around the perimeter."

She almost curtsied, but thought better of it. "Thank you."

"Now, if you would excuse me. I need to show Dark Lord Yates around and introduce him later."

Yesenia smiled at her. "I'll come find you soon. Have fun, Meadow."

Once Khan guided Leo and Yesenia away, she searched for River but noticed he was at a stall with Nora, looking at a kitten with rainbow-colored fur.

Laurie spoke up. "What would you like to do first, Emmy? Dance? Eat? Look at the stalls?"

She tightened her arms around each of theirs. "All of it! I want to do as much as possible."

He chuckled. "As you wish. Let's start with the stalls and wait for a slower dance, so we can all dance together."

"I'm not the best dancer, even with my lessons. So you'd better watch your feet."

Joseph said, "You're far better than you think, love. And with us surrounding you, you won't have to worry about your bracelet, either, and can just fully relax."

Even though Meadow was getting better at controlling her magic without the training bracelet, she'd opted for caution tonight. "Just make sure you two behave during the dance. Especially since I promised to stop by Nadia's family's booth, as well as Helena's sister's one, too. And I don't want to be kicked out for indecency before that."

Laurie whispered, "We'll save that for our properly improper masquerade balls at Nyx's Kingdom."

She smiled. "I can't wait. But for now, I think I see Nadia. So let's head in that direction."

They made their way around the sides of the square, and Meadow kept getting distracted by all of the proudly displayed items, made with and without magic, and how much more charm and character they had versus buying things from giant box stores or massive online platforms. Maybe they treasured things longer here since they were a bigger deal to purchase?

And even though she was tempted, she refrained from buying anything yet, wanting to see her friends first.

She reached Nadia's brother's stall. And even though it belonged to her brother, Nadia stood nearby and was helping out. She waved and came to greet them. "Meadow! You look lovely, and your vampires aren't too bad themselves, either."

"Your dress is stunning. A little different from the rest, but in a good way."

All of them wore flowing dresses, but Nadia's had small shapes embroidered along the hem, sleeves, and bodice. They almost looked like hieroglyphs, but not quite.

She traced some of the shapes along the top of the sleeve. "It's the old fae witch language in Egypt. Few speak it any longer, let alone read it, but my mother loves to embroider it on clothing. And since my brother runs an import business that often sells Egyptian items, ones that he combines with his powers of magical tricks to make things even more memorable for special occasions, it seemed appropriate to wear this."

Meadow had never met a fae witch who had light magic. They were usually referred to as magical tricksters since they could construct light displays that lay dormant until something was opened.

Before she could stop herself, she blurted, "Will he and the others put on a light-work display tonight?"

Nadia nodded. "That's the idea, as long as the weather stays nice. But you don't have to stay here and talk to me all night. Go have fun with your vampires! This is your first fae witch festival, and after all the training you've been doing, you definitely deserve some fun."

"Thank you, Nadia. As long as you promise to have some fun yourself."

"I will. My husband should be around shortly, and then we'll dance."

After saying goodbye, Meadow turned to Laurie and Joseph. "So, what should we do next?"

The music changed to a slower tune, and Joseph smiled. "Speaking of dancing, this is our song. Come on."

Her heart raced as they led her out onto the dance floor. She really wasn't that great of a dancer, and yet she knew how much Laurie and Joseph enjoyed it.

You danced with Joseph at the ball, after all. Trust them. You know you do.

And soon Joseph was behind her, his hands on her waist, as Laurie took her hands. They began the intricate dance of moving and twirling, alternating which person she faced.

They weren't the only trio on the dance floor, and even some older children were dancing, too.

Between the lights overhead, the music, and the laughter all around her, Meadow couldn't remember the last time she'd been so happy. Oh, she loved being naked and in bed with Laurie and Joseph, too. She always would.

But for a girl who'd been in hiding for so long, never getting the chance to experience life, it was magical.

Just as the music died down, someone screamed. Within seconds, a thick, dark smoke rose up from the dance floor.

For a beat, she wondered if it was just part of the theatrics. However, as the other fae witches started shouting and running away, someone crashed into her. Before she could fall, Laurie and Joseph surrounded her, and Laurie asked, "Are you okay?"

"I-I think so." She coughed as the smoke thickened. "What's going on?"

Joseph spoke up. "Given the magical protections, some fae witches invited to the festival must've turned traitor and are attacking."

The smoke, the shouts, and the constant jolting made Meadow's heart race, and she instinctively touched her training bracelet.

You need to keep your emotions in check, as best as you can. Otherwise, you'll make it worse.

She let Laurie and Joseph maneuver her to the edge

of the dance floor, deftly pushing aside anyone who would've run into them.

Meadow focused on breathing, which wasn't easy given the smoke. It thinned a little along the edge of the dance floor, and when she could finally stop coughing, she asked, "Did they do this to go after Khan, Leo, or both?"

Joseph replied, "I'm not sure, but probably both. For now, the most important thing is getting you to safety. After that, we'll go find Leo, Nora, and your siblings."

Laurie spoke up. "I can go and look for my brother and sister by myself. You should stay with Meadow."

Joseph gripped Laurie's shoulder. "No. Our guards can protect her. Everyone thinks we're indulgent, lazy vampires who don't know how to fight, and it might make either of us a target regardless of the truth. Whereas our guards look the part, and will be more of a deterrent."

Laurie grunted. "But you learned to survive on the streets and then taught me. I'd trust you more and can take care of myself."

"It's chaos out there, Laurie. We need to go together to have any chance at all. And the clock's ticking."

Laurie stared for a few seconds before nodding.

The image of either one of them being attacked and something going wrong sent a shiver of fear through her. Meadow gripped both of their arms and stated, "Let me help you guys. I'm sure I can do something with my magic."

Joseph kissed her quickly. "I know you could, love." He gestured behind her. "But the guards are gathering the children and the elderly together, and they need your help and magic more than we do."

Her eyes heated at the thought of him going out there and dying. "No, Joseph."

Laurie cupped her cheek. "No one's magic will work on us with our rings on, and that puts us at an advantage. Remember, vampires are physically stronger than fae witches."

She glanced between them, wanting to argue.

And yet, the growing number of vulnerable fae witches being herded into the great hall made her hesitate.

Joseph said, "They need you, Emmy. We'll send some of our guards as well, to help protect everyone."

Laurie nodded. "Trust us, Emmy. Because coming back to you is a bloody strong motivation to stay alive."

She placed her hand over Laurie's on her cheek, and the other on Joseph's chest. They wanted her to trust them. And maybe a few weeks ago, she would've scoffed.

But now? They'd done everything they'd ever promised, and they knew this time period far better than she.

In other words, Meadow needed to be smart and not let her stubbornness or determination to prove herself put everyone in danger.

Finally, she nodded. "Just promise me that you'll both come back. Since vampires can't lie, that means you'll do everything you can to fulfill it."

Joseph smiled. "Even without a vow, we'd move heaven and earth to be with you. But yes, I promise to come back to you, love."

Laurie spoke up. "Me, too. No matter what, we'll make it back to you."

A tear rolled down her cheek, but she forced herself to say, "Okay. I'll help protect those in the great hall. Just don't do anything stupid."

She wanted to demand that they stay with her. And yet, they were right. She'd stated many times that she could protect herself, and if she could also save the children, she would.

Unless the enemies have protection rings or bracelets on.

As if reading her thoughts, Laurie slipped a small pistol into her hand. "This is magically infused to hit threats to your life. It won't miss, and it'll give you time to get away."

More tears threatened to fall, but she willed them away. She could do this. She *had* to do this.

She took the gun. "If you see River, help him, too."

Joseph touched her cheek. "Of course."

Laurie placed a hand on her lower back. "Come on. Let's get you safe inside with the guards and children. I think I see Helena there as well."

As they reached the entrance to the building, Joseph kissed her, and then Laurie, before both stepped away. Laurie winked at her. "Until later, my love. I expect to be rewarded handsomely for my bravery."

Joseph rolled his eyes, but before Meadow could reply, they both gestured toward the great hall at her back. They watched until she was inside, then they disappeared into the smoke.

She didn't have time to be sad or dwell on what-ifs because in less than a minute, Meadow was overseeing a large group of children and the elderly, with more fae witch guards around the perimeter than she could count.

Helena was also inside, speaking with one of the guards, as were some of the fae witch council.

She played with her training bracelet and kept an eye on the door. Part of her wanted to storm out and help Laurie and Joseph.

And yet, the rational part of her brain knew she didn't have enough control over her powers to be of help in such dangerous circumstances.

But if it came to it, she'd do whatever it took to protect those who couldn't protect themselves. And so she went over to Helena to see what she could do, and then readied herself for battle.

Chapter Twenty-Three

Laurie didn't like leaving Meadow in the care of others. However, she didn't have anything to protect against magical powers, like him and Joseph. Plus, this was the fae witch territory, and their guards would better know how to fight against magic, if it came to it.

Even though Laurie didn't have magic, his advantages were strength and weapons. If a fae witch couldn't use their magic against him, they became vulnerable. And he hoped it would be enough to survive.

No, it *had* to be enough. Not just to ensure Meadow's safety, but his brother was also out there somewhere in this chaos. While he wanted to save his brother because he loved him, he also had no desire to step up and lead the vampires of London, which his family had done for centuries.

As if reading his thoughts, Joseph leaned close and

said, "Our first task is finding Leo and Khan. If something happens to either of them, it'll ignite a war. One that'll be far more dangerous to Emmy and all those we care about."

"If we find Nora, I'm helping her, no matter if we haven't found Khan or Leo, though."

"Of course. But as hard as it'll be, we can't save them all right now, Laurie. Please tell me you understand that."

"I don't like it, but I know. And I'm definitely going to have a word with Khan later. So much for protecting his territory."

"We'll think about that later, once we discover who is responsible. For now, we need to watch each other's backs and look for the leaders, your sister, and River."

He nodded, and just like they'd done during their days on the streets, they each kept an eye on one side, ready to alert the other of any oncoming threat.

The previously happy and magical dance floor was gone, replaced by people running around or lying unconscious on the ground. As much as he wanted to check on them all, more would get hurt, or worse, if they couldn't find the bastards who'd attacked and stop the threat.

So he forced himself to ignore the injured, trusting the others to take care of them, and tightened his grip on the pistol in one hand and the blade in the other. Since he and Joseph wore magical protection rings, their biggest threat was a physical ambush.

A sound of grunting garnered his attention, and he made out some shapes on the stage. He focused until he could see Leo and River trying to take down a fae witch with glowing hands. Nora was huddled as far back on the platform as she could go, her hands crossed protectively over her pregnant belly.

The sight snapped something inside Laurie. This time, he would help Nora. Never again would he allow her to be hurt.

After motioning to Joseph, he rushed the stage and jumped up. The fae witch with the glowing hands reached for him, but Laurie thrust his knife into the male's chest, and he stumbled backward. The glow faded as the fae witch crumbled to the ground.

Leo breathed heavily as River went to Nora. Leo said, "Thanks, Laurie."

Laurie retrieved his knife—the fae witch was dead—and nodded. "Maybe now you'll listen to me about wearing a magic protection ring and ignore anyone who thinks it makes you look weak. But where's Yesenia?"

"She was a few stalls ahead with Khan when the fighting broke out. Nora was in trouble, and Yesenia knows how to handle herself with her time-travel magic. She probably has them all in nets or something by now, and Khan probably has them clawing their eyes out to stop the nightmares."

River nodded at Laurie and Joseph as he asked, "Where's Meadow?"

Joseph replied, "She's in the great hall, along with the children, the elderly, and quite a few guards. It's probably the safest place right now, until all of this dies down."

River tightened his hold on Nora as he said, "We'll head there, then. I can help heal the injured and better look after Nora."

The sight of his sister, pale and leaning heavily against River, set off warning bells. "Are you okay, Nora? And the baby?"

River spoke first. "I already did a quick check while we were talking, but everything seems fine." He hugged Nora a little tighter. "I might need to borrow a gun from you two, though, to be able to make it to the great hall safely."

Laurie gestured toward Leo. "You should go with them, Leo. Joseph and I will find Yesenia."

Leo growled. "No fucking way. One of you go with River and Nora. I'm going to find my wife." Leo wiped his brow, took the pistol offered by Joseph, and then motioned with his head. "She should be that way."

Laurie shared a look with Joseph, who clearly didn't want to leave him alone. He leaned over to Joseph's ear and whispered, "Look after my sister and Meadow. There's no one I trust more."

He kissed him, and Joseph sighed. "Fine. But if you fucking die, I'm going to bring you back to life so I can strangle you myself."

Laurie winked. "Deal."

After staring at each other for another second, they parted ways. Laurie kept up with Leo, and only when they were about five feet away from Yesenia and Khan could he see them.

"Fuck," Laurie muttered.

Yesenia was alone, objects falling and hitting those

around her, standing over an unconscious Khan on the ground.

He said to Leo, "I'll go left and you go right. We need to get them both out of here, and fast."

And so he and Leo went into the fray, fighting to get to Yesenia and Khan's side. There were a hell of a lot of people to defeat, and Laurie wondered why so many fae witches had turned against their own kind, given the reports of them being content with Khan's leadership.

Then something sliced his arm, and he focused, drawing on his remaining strength. The sooner he took care of these threats, the sooner he could go back to Meadow and Joseph.

Meadow had learned from Helena that something was blocking her tracking powers. Well, for whoever had attacked. Helena could still locate and identify every person in the hall, or even the attendees outside.

And since there was only one way to avoid a powerful tracker's abilities—magical hexes that used forbidden arts and cost a small fortune—it meant that some of Khan's fae witches had turned traitor.

However, for the moment, Meadow focused on helping those in the great hall and taking care of minor injuries. No one inside the meeting hall had strong healing powers, so they were relying on the old methods of cleaning and dressing and stitching wounds.

Even if she didn't enjoy the sight of blood, she pushed through. It was the least she could do, considering Laurie and Joseph were outside fighting against who knew how many enemies.

A new wave of refugees was allowed inside by the guards, and as soon as Meadow saw River and Nora, along with Joseph, a mixture of relief and fear rushed through her.

Where was Laurie?

She murmured her excuses and rushed over into Joseph's arms. "Where's Laurie?"

He rubbed her back. "He's helping Leo find and rescue Yesenia and Khan."

"Will he be okay?"

Joseph said, "Yes. Remember, Yesenia is strong in her own right, as is Khan. And whilst Leo might be a Dark Lord now, he spent twenty years in the army. Not to mention Laurie spent years on the streets with me, and I taught him everything he knows. You need to trust him, love."

Trust Laurie. That's all you can do right now. So even though a million questions raced through her head, she forced herself to focus on River and Nora. "Are you two all right?"

Nora looked paler than normal, but she still nodded. "Just a bit rattled. However, River already confirmed that both me and the baby are fine." She gestured around the room. "Joseph said there are a lot of injured people, and we want to help. So tell us what you need."

Leave it to Nora to think of others when she'd just

gone through something traumatic herself. Meadow replied, "Well, there are lots of minor injuries and a few broken bones, but no one here has any strong healing magic, and they could definitely use River's powers. However, if you two need a few moments to gather yourselves, I think everyone would understand."

River shook his head. "No need. As long as Nora sits near me while I heal and doesn't overdo it, I can help whoever needs it."

Meadow reached out and gripped River's hand. "You're amazing, brother."

A faint glimmer of his charm came through as he said, "I know it. Now, tell me what's been done so far for the worst cases."

She released his hand and replied, "Helena used her power of persuasion to calm and help those with the worst pain. But while no one has become hysterical yet, they're mostly still in shock, and I worry about what'll happen when it fades." She lowered her voice. "The most worrying thing, though, is that Helena can't tell who attacked." She explained about the dark arts and something hiding them from her powers before adding, "If there are any details you can share with her as you heal people, that would be extremely helpful."

River replied, "Of course. Now, show me those with the worst injuries first."

Meadow reluctantly let go of Joseph. "Sure. But first—you should go help Laurie, Joseph."

"He's with Leo. And as much as I want to be the hero, going back out there alone is a death sentence. Plus, I promised Laurie to look after you."

He caressed her cheek, and she leaned into the touch. "Is Leo that good of a fighter, then?"

Joseph nodded. "He led the team that rescued his nephew, Ambrose, after all."

Meadow had heard the story, although she rarely saw Ambrose himself. If they all survived this, she needed to get to know her future nephew.

Not if. No, *when* they survived this. "Then I'll trust him."

Joseph stroked her cheek. "Good. Whilst you help your brother, I'll work with the guards to protect the doors." He patted his jacket. "I still have a few tricks of my own, and I can't wait to use them."

She knew she needed to leave him and help those in pain. However, it was on the tip of her tongue to say she loved him—she loved them both. And yet, she held back. Now wasn't the time. After touching his jaw, she said, "I trust you. But make sure to let me know if anything changes, okay?"

"I will, love. I promise."

He kissed her, and she reluctantly went to help River. And as she coaxed the injured to stay calm with her secondary persuasion magic, she and River made quick work of healing those who needed it.

She and her brother were approaching the newest refugees when the door disintegrated and light flared, blinding them all.

Once it died down, she blinked until she could finally make out a tall male with blond hair holding Helena and pressing a glowing knife against her throat. He pricked her skin, and she instantly went slack.

Meadow lunged forward, but the male's booming voice —aided by dark magic—filled the space. "Take another step, and not only will she die a slower death, I'll kill you too."

She stilled and instinctively gathered magic into her chest. She'd removed her training bracelet to help the injured, and maybe, just maybe, she could use her powers of lust and desire to stop the madman and his companions.

Because those who resorted to the dark arts couldn't use magic protection items. If they did, it would cancel out any dark hexes inked into their skin.

However, to have any chance of success, Meadow needed enough magic to release her strongest spell ever. Given the dark aura and signs of dark arts visible on the male's hands, he'd be harder to manipulate than the average fae witch.

If at all, rushed through her head.

Pushing aside her doubts, she began to weave a tight net, one she could toss over the leader. Him going down would create enough confusion to give the others a chance to help her.

For a split second, she wondered where Joseph was. But to worry would affect her magic, so she pushed it aside and continued making her net until she thought it was good enough to place over the leader. She did, carefully, and he flinched. His eyes zeroed in on hers, glowed a dark red, and he tossed Helena aside and stalked toward her. "I warned you about what would happen. You die first."

A cry came from the door, and Laurie and Joseph

crashed inside. The male sliced his hand through the air, and a table rose and flew backward, hitting the pair and sending them against the wall. A loud crack filled the room before they thudded to the ground.

They didn't move.

Pushing aside her fear and the need to go to them, Meadow focused on the anger coursing through her—how dare he hurt her vampires. He needed to pay.

She would try one more time to control the leader, and this time, she wouldn't be careful. No, she would fully embrace her powers and let go, giving him everything she had. She was a motherfucking Wielder, after all.

And if she could get the other fae witches to use their powers to help distract him? It should give her a few extra seconds to focus so she could attack again.

She shouted, "Use whatever magic you have to help me!"

Persuasion magic filled the air, and others began dancing fire, and water, and even light around the room. Some of the lesser intruders turned ill or changed into frogs or even shimmered, as if they were fading from existence.

Anger and love and determination swirled inside her. She was ready.

Drawing in as much magic as she could, she screamed, "Lust after your fellow traitors, embrace and hold each other, never allowing them to flee. Writhe on the ground and become too aroused to move!"

Unleashing her magic, she let it free, aiming it at their enemies.

For a beat, nothing changed.

Then they began clutching their dicks over their trousers, lunging for one another, and holding each other to the ground, to keep them from running away.

"Anyone able, help restrain and capture the traitors!"

Various fae witch guards stumbled to their feet and attacked the intruders. Magic and knives and pistols were used in a flurry. The adults were shielding the children as best they could. Meadow wished she could save them the scene, but saving their lives was more important.

As the enemies were taken down, including their leader, Meadow rushed to Laurie and Joseph's sides.

They were still, so still.

But then she saw the slow rise and fall of their chests, and she sobbed. They were still breathing, which meant they were alive.

Looking around for River, she saw him helping Helena, who was now sitting up and holding her head.

"River! If she's healed already, come help Laurie and Joseph! Please!"

She focused back on her two males, kissing each of their cheeks and murmuring, "You'd better wake up again. I love you both and want to tell you. There's so much more to our story, and I refuse to believe it ends here."

River arrived, and he placed a hand on each male as he performed his magical examination. He met her gaze, and she didn't like the mixture of resolve and worry there. "I need to heal them. Now. One has a broken spine, and the other a massive head injury."

Meadow swallowed a sob. "Tell me what to do."

"Use your persuasion to keep them here with us."

A series of bells rang outside, and Meadow looked around for more enemies.

River answered, "That's the all-clear. The threats are contained."

Maybe for the evening, but as she stared at Laurie and Joseph, the threat of losing the future she wanted was still there. "Then let's get started. Help them, River. Please."

He nodded, looked as if he was about to say something, but then focused on healing Joseph first—who had the brain injury. River's hands glowed as Meadow whispered right between Laurie and Joseph, "You two will live. You had better. There's so much more to our future. But to be happy and finally embrace all of who I am, I need you two. You're my everything. I love you."

And she put her faith in her brother's abilities, unable to think about what would happen if he failed.

But as her heart calmed and the adrenaline faded from her body, the room tilted before going black.

Chapter Twenty-Four

Joseph sat next to Meadow's bed, holding her hand, and willed for her to open her eyes.

According to River, her saving the day had come at a cost—magical burnout.

She'd pushed her magic beyond her limits, and now she faced an internal battle none of them could see. And if she didn't overcome it, then she'd never wake up.

It'd been two days since the disastrous festival. Khan was doing damage control and using every iota of magic he possessed to get answers out of the still-living traitors.

Apparently, one of Yesenia's weapons—a brick—had been tossed back at Khan during the battle, knocking him unconscious. The fae witch male was as cool as ever, but at least he didn't hold any ill will toward Yesenia. Plus, Leo fighting to save Khan had gone a long way toward the fae witches beginning to trust the new vampire Dark Lord.

Joseph was fully healed now, and although Laurie's spine was mending and he'd make a full recovery, it would take time to get there and he currently relied on a wheelchair.

For the time being, they were inside Dark Lord Khan's residence. Not only for safety concerns but also because it held rare texts that River was looking through to try and find a way to help his sister.

Joseph brushed some hair off Meadow's forehead and murmured, "Come on, love. Wake up for us. After everything that happened, it put things into perspective, and we want you with us. Forever. But first, you need to wake up."

Silence.

As he debated fetching Laurie to come sit with them, River rushed into the room. His hair was mussed, a two-day-old beard was on his face, and the dark circles under his eyes signaled he hadn't slept much.

But in the next second, Joseph forgot about that as River blurted, "I think I found a way to help her." He held up a book and continued, "According to this, it requires your and Laurie's help."

He frowned. "What are you talking about? Tell me the details, River. Plainly."

"Since Meadow is still your unclaimed fated one, you and Laurie possess a little magic that will react with hers. Namely, if you each take a small bit of her blood, you should hallucinate and see what she sees right now.

The book is vague about whether you can communicate with her in the hallucination or not. However, at this point, anything that might help Meadow is worth a shot."

Joseph willed himself not to get hopeful. Yet. "What magic are you talking about? Full-blooded vampires don't have magic."

"Ah, but they do. All of you do. It's a lingering result of the original curse put on your kind."

He blinked. "That's real?"

"Apparently. Thankfully, Khan let me scour his forbidden texts and said we could use this information to help Meadow. Although, obviously, you can't share it with anyone else or Khan will arrest you."

He tightened his grip on Meadow's hand. "Of course we won't tell anyone. But is Laurie strong enough to help? Or can I just do it by myself?"

"No, it has to be the fated one or ones, which means in this case it has to be the both of you. That connection is what will trigger the hallucinations. There's more to it all, of course, but that's the gist of it. As for Laurie, he should be fine as long as he listens to his body and acknowledges his limits. Normally, I'd wait another few days. But in this case…"

Joseph looked back at Meadow's pale face. "If we wait much longer, she might never wake up."

"Exactly."

A knock at the door made him turn around, and he saw Nora wheeling Laurie inside. Judging by the determined look on his face, Nora or River had already explained the situation.

Laurie nodded. "I'm doing it because we can't afford to wait. The thought of Meadow losing everything after she finally accepted herself makes me both sad and angry. I won't let those arseholes traitors take that from her. From us."

Nora stopped Laurie on the opposite side of the bed and spoke up. "Another healer is staying in Khan's residence, too, in case we need her. River has barely slept over the last two days, and he might not be well enough to help with anything serious."

River grunted. "I would argue, but she's right. I can do minor things, but Meadow might need more. For now, let me go over what you need to do, and then we'll get started."

And as he explained the steps needed to maybe join Meadow's hallucinations and convince her to wake up, Joseph listened to every detail. Because he refused to make a mistake and risk Meadow's life.

Meadow was locked in a dark, humid basement. Only a single flickering candle kept the worst of her fears at bay.

They'd tossed her inside the magical rogue prison, blaming her for making things worse at the fae witch festival.

She hadn't helped.

She hadn't saved the day.

And Laurie and Joseph were dead.

She sat on the ground and hugged her knees closer

to her chest. So much for doing better and not being the fuckup her father had always accused her of being.

If she had any tears left, she'd cry some more. But she'd cried until she was hoarse, and she struggled to stay awake.

But she didn't want to sleep. The last time she'd tried, all she'd dreamed about were Laurie and Joseph's lifeless bodies.

Their eyes open, staring at nothing, as they lay unmoving and pale.

All because of me.

The door opened, and Meadow jumped a little. The figure in the doorway looked like Yesenia, but she had white streaks in her hair. Her eyes were also hard and cruel, with no sign of affection or warmth.

Although could she really blame her? Maybe Meadow had also hurt or failed Leo. The darkness-clad guards had refused to tell her anything.

As Yesenia narrowed her eyes, Meadow's stomach dropped. *Oh, no. Please don't let River be hurt, or worse, because of me.*

Before she could go down the road of what-ifs, the not-quite-Yesenia stated, "I'm sending you back to the future to our father. I never should've brought you here. Because of you, River and Nora are dead."

Fear shot through her. "No!"

Yesenia walked in and stopped to spit on her. "You killed them."

She snapped her fingers, and in the next instant, Meadow was in her old bedroom at her father's place, except there were bars on the windows and the door had changed into a metal door with bars, like a jail cell.

Her father appeared at the door, tossed a bottle of water into the room, and said, "Lose another forty pounds and agree to my plan, and maybe I'll let you outside for an hour. But for now, I can't stand the disgusting sight of you. How you ever came from Maribelle, I have no idea."

He walked away. Meadow tried to get up, but she was too weak to do more than raise a hand.

The eerie silence allowed Yesenia's words to repeat in her mind—River and Nora were dead. All because Meadow had tried to save the day when she hadn't been strong enough.

She'd been an utter failure.

Again.

She sobbed and struggled to breathe. She'd killed her brother and his kind wife.

What had she done?

Maybe she should stop fighting and just refuse to eat anything. Maybe then she'd stop hurting everyone she cared about.

"Meadow," a male voice whispered. And then another. "Love, can you hear us?"

It sounded like Laurie and Joseph.

But, no. They were dead. And even if they weren't, they'd want nothing to do with her, either. She'd killed Laurie's sister.

"Damn it, Meadow, come to us. We need to talk."

She should ignore the whispering voices, turn inward, and wait for death.

"Meadow," they kept whispering.

Just the sound of their voices made her heart break even further. Were they haunting her?

If so, then the last thing she could do for them was to let them yell and shout and berate her for failing them. Maybe then they'd get enough peace to finally leave the world.

Yes, she would listen, no matter how painful it was.

The room changed again, and this time she was inside her bedroom at Nyx's Kingdom, back in the past. Laurie and Joseph strode through the door, and her heart ached at how handsome they were.

She expected hatred or disgust in their eyes. However, she blinked at the concern.

What was going on?

They walked up to her bed, each taking a side before gripping one of her hands. She was weak but could move her head from side to side, and became even more confused at their tender looks. "What's going on? Why aren't you mad at me?" she croaked.

Worry flashed in Laurie's eyes before he replied, "We're here for you, Meadow. To give you strength and help you fight this battle."

Joseph jumped in. "None of this is real—you burned out. All of this is fake, constructed by your own mind to make you give up."

She shook her head. "No, I must be imagining you. Everyone is dead. You're dead. You're both dead."

Her voice cracked on the last word as a tear trailed down her cheek. Laurie quickly wiped it away. "We're alive, Emmy. We're here because of the bond we share.

We're here to convince you to wake up so we can marry you."

For a beat, Meadow's heart warmed, and she wished it were true.

But then she pushed the hope aside. "No. It's a dream, just a dream. Please just leave me to die."

Joseph leaned down, cupped her cheek, and kissed her. Gently at first, but then it turned fierce. When he broke it, they both breathed heavily. He murmured, "We're alive, love. We all are. Thanks to you."

"No, I didn't save anyone."

"You did. And if you wake up, you'll see, Emmy. But you have to fight because only you can end this nightmare."

Laurie turned her head toward him and laid his forehead against hers. His hot breath against her lips made her yearn for him to be still alive. For him and Joseph to hold her, want her, and love her.

But they were gone. Forever. And even dreaming about them made her heart ache.

Before she found the strength to tell them to leave her alone, Laurie whispered, "I love you, Meadow Vale. Please believe us and fight to wake up. You're burned out, and this is all a hallucination determined to make you lose hope. And deep down, I think you know I speak the truth. Remember what happened to your mother."

Images of her mother being unconscious for days flashed through her mind. And even when her mom eventually woke up because of an experimental treatment—used to shock fae witches awake—she'd walked around like a ghost.

Not long after, she'd jumped off a building.

Could she be experiencing the same thing?

Joseph whispered into her ear, "I love you as well, Meadow Vale. Please fight and wake up. Everyone's waiting to see you again. You helped save the day, and so many want to say thank you."

Doubt crept into her mind. Could it be true? Was this a burnout hallucination meant to make her feel hopeless?

Or were Laurie and Joseph the hallucination, one she'd conjured to make her feel less defeated?

Laurie and Joseph lay down on either side of her, and laid their arms across her body, holding her tight.

They were warm and familiar, and they made her feel safe and wanted.

Maybe it was all fake. But for now, for however long they were here, she desperately wanted to believe them.

"Love you too."

Their arms tightened a little across her, and they each kissed a cheek.

And even if she were wrong and woke up later to discover her vampires had been a dream, Meadow snuggled into their warmth and willed for them to be speaking the truth. That she'd wake up and find everyone still alive.

She drifted off into nothingness.

"Meadow. Open your eyes, Meadow. You can do it."

The voice sounded like…River.

"Did she just move a hand?"

"I think so."

"Come on, Emmy. Just a little more and you'll be back with us."

And now Laurie, Joseph, and Nora had just spoken to her?

All the people she'd thought she'd killed?

Determined to see if she were imagining things, Meadow struggled to open her eyes. However, her eyelids weighed a ton, and she couldn't do it.

Then she felt someone—or two someones—squeezing her hands.

Even without seeing them, she knew it was Laurie and Joseph.

Her heart ached to see them again. So she used the last of her energy, and dim lighting finally greeted her eyes.

She blinked a few times, and Laurie, Joseph, River, and Nora came into focus.

Laurie grinned, and Joseph briefly closed his eyes. They both leaned down on the bed, to better make eye contact.

Joseph spoke first. "Welcome back, love."

Laurie said, "That means now you'll have to marry us."

Joseph sighed. "Give her some time to regain her strength before you say things like that."

Laurie quirked an eyebrow. "No. We nearly lost her, and I'm not waiting for anything."

Meadow's head buzzed as she tried to take it all in. "Is this real, or am I dreaming again?"

"It's real, pet." And Laurie kissed her.

"You burned out, but now you're back with us. Where you belong." He also kissed her.

She glanced between the pair as hope gathered in her chest. Was this reality and not the bleak one?

However, before she could reply, River said, "You were unconscious for over two days, Em. But now you're back, and I need to disturb your reunion to examine you."

"River," she said with a sob. "I thought you were dead."

He smiled and shook his head. "No, Em. I'm right here. If this were a dream or hallucination, I'm sure that I wouldn't look like a sleep-deprived hermit."

She laughed, actually laughed, and said, "This has to be real. That's only something you'd say, River."

He snorted. "Well, glad to be of service." He gestured at Laurie and Joseph. "You two need to let us examine her. While you wait, maybe you can think of a better way to propose to my little sister because your first try was pretty shitty."

They both gave him the double-finger salute before focusing back on Meadow. Laurie and Joseph each kissed the back of a hand before murmuring they'd be back.

However, as soon as they released her hands and stepped back, panic raced through her. She cried out, "Don't go! Please don't go."

River's face filled her vision. Her poor brother looked ragged. He said, "They'll be just outside the door, Em. You're out of immediate danger, but I need to make sure your brain is healing from the burnout."

An unfamiliar fae witch entered and nodded at River before he continued, "This is Stella. She also has healing magic, and will help me determine if anything else is wrong. Please let us take care of you, Meadow."

At the pleading in his voice, no doubt a result of him also remembering what had happened to their mother, Meadow softened. "Of course, River. As long as Laurie and Joseph come back as soon as possible. I need to answer their proposal, after all."

River sighed dramatically. "You're going to say yes, aren't you? And then I'll have to deal with them all the time."

Nora shook her head and said, "You like them both, so stop pretending you don't." She smiled at Meadow. "I'll keep Laurie and Joseph company and bring them right back, I promise, Meadow. I'm so happy you're with us again, too."

With that, Nora herded them out of the room, and Meadow let her brother and the other fae witch doctor examine her.

Her heart raced the whole time, but not from some lingering burnout effects. No, it raced because she wanted to give Laurie and Joseph her answer.

Because of course she would marry them. After thinking she'd lost them forever, she didn't want to waste another minute apart from them. Ever.

Chapter Twenty-Five

Nearly a week later, Laurie stood with Joseph at the front of a small ballroom inside Khan's residence, waiting for Meadow to appear.

It was their wedding day.

His family members, Meadow's new friends, and a few of their friends from Nyx's Kingdom sat in chairs, dressed up and smiling, looking at the door, eager for the ceremony to begin.

Meadow had said yes to their proposal. And since the only way Khan would allow Laurie and Joseph to take her back to the vampire territory was to wed her, they'd all readily agreed.

Over the last week, Khan had interrogated the traitors and found out that Helena's ex-fiancé had been the leader. He'd taken her rejection seriously, and when approached by the French vampires and offered a large sum of money, had rushed to recruit as many people as possible. Not only to get revenge on Helena, but also to betray Khan, who'd refused to side with the ex over the broken marriage promise. Unlike humans, fae witch females had nearly equal rights in London—especially for those with powers as strong as Helena Watts.

The fae witch Dark Lord was also tracking down those who'd used their forbidden dark arts on the traitors to circumvent the protection spells and trigger traps. Khan had assured Laurie that the same hexes wouldn't work on his residence since the protection spells were older, far more powerful, and the building held other secrets he couldn't reveal.

There was more behind the festival attacks, Laurie was sure of it, but Khan wasn't sharing. Well, at least with the public, or Laurie and Joseph. No doubt Leo knew more of the truth. However, if there were a threat to any of them, Leo would keep them updated. Just as he'd revealed the trap at the Fated Wheel had been successful, and Leo would share more after his, Joseph's, and Meadow's marriage.

Until then, he'd have to trust his brother with all the politics and strategizing and spying.

Music began playing, and Laurie pushed everything else out of his mind as Meadow appeared in the doorway.

His heart skipped a beat at how gorgeous she was. Her dress hugged her breasts before flaring outward. Her hair was twisted up, highlighting the ear cuffs he and Joseph had given her.

But it was her smile that was breathtaking. When combined with the love shining in her eyes, he couldn't believe how lucky he was that she would be their wife.

And to think they'd nearly lost her.

Joseph took his hand and squeezed, as if thinking the same thing and needing to reassure himself as much as Laurie.

She never took her gaze from either him or Joseph, and sooner than he expected, she stood between them. Then the three of them formed a circle, clasping hands, and the officiant began speaking.

"We're gathered here today to join these three in marriage, to bond them with the law as much as they are already bonded together in love. If anyone objects to this union, then speak now or forever hold your peace."

Silence. Thankfully, nothing but silence.

The ceremony proceeded, and Laurie barely noticed anything apart from the feel of Meadow and Joseph's hands in his. Well, and the bit where they all exchanged rings.

Far too soon the fae witch officiant declared them a marriage triad, husbands and wife, and the three of them gave a quick three-way kiss.

The more passionate version would happen later in the bedroom, when Laurie and Joseph finally claimed Meadow with their fangs and cocks.

He and Joseph each offered Meadow an arm before heading back down the aisle, and everyone cheered. Laurie's heart thudded, and he willed himself not to cry. He was happy, so unbelievably happy, to the point he felt he'd burst.

Once they were in the hallway, he and Joseph guided Meadow to a shielded corner and held her between them. Oh, they still had to sit through a celebratory feast. But he just wanted to hold his husband and wife close, and revel in them being together.

Of them beginning the future he'd always dreamed of.

Meadow had never wanted their private moment of holding each other to end. In Laurie and Joseph's arms, and with them in hers, she felt safe. Whole. Complete.

And loved. So thoroughly loved.

However, Yesenia and River eventually found them and herded them to their wedding reception being held down the hall.

Somehow she endured the next few hours of congratulations and toasts and dances. Even though their wedding was a small affair, she didn't care. Her siblings and new in-laws were there, as were Helena's and Nadia's families. Even a few familiar faces from Nyx's Kingdom, such as Frank and Susanna, had been allowed to attend. Khan had made a brief appearance, merely nodding his approval and wishing them well, before returning to the task of finding those who'd financed Helena's ex and the other traitors.

The depth of betrayal from their fellow fae witches had rocked the territory and its people. The only good thing to come from it all was that they now viewed Leo as an ally instead of a threat. Meadow was glad, although the next few weeks would be too hectic for her to think much about Leo and Khan's alliance. Between being newly married and planning on how to better protect Nyx's Kingdom and those they cared about, she, Laurie, and Joseph would be busy.

And while she hadn't forgotten about the unknown threats to any of them, they'd all agreed that for today, their wedding, they would have fun, live in the present, and make memories to last a lifetime.

As Laurie and Joseph escorted her off the dance floor for the fourth or fifth time, she couldn't stop smiling. Sure, her feet hurt and her hair had started to fall out of its pins, but she was happy. Her family was here, her new friends, and ever since waking up from her burnout, she'd never had a problem controlling her powers. Almost as if the internal fear and mental blocks had vanished once she'd helped capture the traitors.

Laurie and Joseph guided her toward the door. She glanced at one of her husbands and then the other as she asked, "Where are we going now?"

Joseph smiled. "Where do you think?"

She glanced over her shoulder. "Shouldn't we say goodbye or something?"

Laurie shook his head. "Let them celebrate and enjoy themselves. If we formally take our leave, they might feel obligated to stop."

She arched an eyebrow. "I'm sure that's the main reason."

He grinned. "It's part of the reason, at least."

Joseph chuckled. "Believe it or not, I'm the one who suggested we sneak out, not Laurie."

Meadow replied, "He's being a bad influence on you, Joseph."

Laurie said, "Now, now, be nice. It's our wedding day. Besides, you've been eager for the claiming as much as we have, Emmy. And you were the one to suggest waiting until the wedding, which was ridiculous considering we've pleasured you many times over by this point."

She lifted her chin. "It wasn't because I was a prude or anything. River suggested that if I waited until today, then I would be strong enough to have you both bite me at once."

Joseph ran a hand down her back until he could possessively grip her butt. "Oh, really? And here I thought River would rather you remain chaste forever than imagine you with us."

She scrunched her nose. "Ew, no, my brother wasn't thinking of *that.* But he knows how important claimings are for vampires, and despite his grumblings, he likes the pair of you."

Laurie wrapped an arm around her shoulders. "How about we stop discussing your brother and walk faster? Khan gave us a room with magically imbued walls, so no one will hear anything, and I'm eager to unwrap my bride."

"Are you going to happy-cry or something, as you unwrap me?" She teased.

Laurie stuck out his tongue. "No, pet. More like you'll be screaming our names."

A rush of heat shot through her. "Yes, please."

Joseph chuckled. "Don't worry, we'll take care of you, love."

They arrived at the door of their honeymoon suite, and Meadow reached for the door handle. However, Joseph stepped in front of her and shook his head. "No, we'll carry you."

Before she could say a word, Joseph swept her into his arms and walked into the room. Once the door was closed, Laurie took her into his arms and carried her to a large bedroom off to the side.

As he slowly put her down, Joseph stood behind Laurie, his gaze heated, as he ran his hands down Laurie's chest to his crotch. Watching Laurie suck in a breath only made Meadow hotter.

Maybe later, or tomorrow, she'd tease and play and ask them to take it slow. But staring at Laurie's fangs and then Joseph's, her core pulsed. She wanted to feel a vampire's bite; the ones when she'd been unconscious didn't count.

She turned around. "Help me out of this dress quickly. And no, that doesn't mean rip it off. I want to keep it."

Laurie moved in front of her and started plucking the pins out of her hair while Joseph undid the buttons at her back. The dress fell down, her hair cascaded over her shoulders, and the pair made quick work of her undergarments.

In record time, she stood naked, with both of her husbands caressing her body and making her ache for more than their fingers.

Laurie kissed her as Joseph removed his hands, and

clothes flew to the floor. Then he turned her toward him, as Laurie did the same.

Once they were all naked, Meadow stepped back to admire one male and then the other before sighing contentedly. "I'm so lucky."

Joseph chuckled. "As are we. Ready for the claiming, love?"

She twirled before jumping onto the bed. "Ready!"

They both grinned at her. But as soon as they crawled onto the mattress and kneeled to either side of her, her smile faded as her heart raced.

Joseph traced her cheek, her jaw, and then ran his finger up and down her neck. "I can't wait to taste your sweet blood, Emmy. The small taste from when we helped you during your burnout has made me crave more every hour of every day."

As his finger continued to caress her, Laurie kissed the other side of her neck before running his fang across her skin, but never breaking it. He murmured, "Tell us we can start. I promise we'll tease and draw out every touch and orgasm later. But right now? I want to taste you, pet. Taste your blood again."

They each cupped one of her breasts and tweaked a nipple. Meadow sucked in a breath before replying, "Yes, please. We have the rest of our lives to explore and tease and be adventurous. Right now, I just want both of you inside me and to finally feel your fangs in my skin."

Joseph released her breast and played with her core. "Nice and wet for us, love." He lay on his back and then stroked his dick. Slowly.

Meadow licked her lips, more than ready to claim her vampire as much as he wanted to claim her.

Joseph stated, "Come here, love. Take me inside you."

She moved to straddle Joseph's hips, and then slowly lowered onto his long, hard cock. She sucked in a breath once she finally took him to the hilt.

Laurie was behind her, ran his hands up Joseph's legs and paused to caress his hips before moving his fingers to Meadow's clit. Laurie nuzzled her neck as he murmured, "Let's put your training to good use, pet."

She leaned forward, and Laurie caressed her rosebud with his thumb coated in something slick. He toyed with her hole, and thanks to their Victorian sex toys and some practice, she easily relaxed as he played with her.

Joseph kissed her as Laurie continued to massage her. Then his thumb was gone, and he gently pushed his cock inside her.

Bit by bit he filled her, until he was fully inside her ass, and Meadow groaned. The two of them together pushed her to the limit, and yet it felt good. So damn good.

Laurie caressed her shoulder as Joseph lifted a hand to touch Laurie's face.

For nearly a minute, they lay there, entwined and touching, until Meadow relaxed and was used to them both inside her.

Joseph grunted. "Nearly there, love. Let's get you closer to *la petite mort* and then we'll claim you with our fangs as well."

She nodded, and both Laurie and Joseph started a rhythm that almost felt like too much, and yet, so, so good.

The pleasure built, little by little, until she was moaning and asking them to go faster, and then her orgasm crashed over her. Wave after wave, so intense she thought maybe she would die.

Then she felt Laurie lean down just as Joseph lifted his head, and they both sank their fangs into her neck, and an even more intense orgasm shot through her. She screamed, arching as much as she could between them, and just as she started to feel a little lightheaded, they released her neck and licked the wounds closed.

She collapsed, and the males both breathed heavily. Laurie lay on her back, bracing most of his weight on his hands on the bed, and Joseph had wrapped his arms around her and Laurie.

They lay like that for at least a minute, until Laurie finally pulled out of her. Too boneless to move, she allowed him to use a warm washcloth on her before guiding her off of Joseph and cleaning her yet again with a fresh one.

Then Laurie and Joseph held her between them and snuggled under the blanket.

She wanted to say something, but all she could manage was, "Mmm."

Laurie chuckled before kissing her forehead. "You have about as much energy as I do, pet."

She snuggled more against them both and yawned. "I love you both, and we're far from done, but I need a nap after that."

Joseph's voice was tinged with worry as he asked, "Did we take too much blood?"

"No, I don't think so. It's been a long day, though, and after that orgasm, I need some time to recover. And you're both so warm that I can't keep my eyes open."

Joseph nuzzled her cheek. "Sleep, Emmy."

"Tell me first."

She felt his smile against her skin. "I love you, Emmy. And I love you, Laurie."

Laurie held them both a little tighter. "I love you, Emmy. And I love you, Joseph."

She smiled and sighed. "Now, let's sleep, and we'll celebrate some more afterward."

And as Meadow drifted off, she barely remembered how this ending had really started in her bedroom back in the future, when she'd had to fend off intruders and run for her life.

Little had she known that she'd been running toward her future and the happy ending she'd never thought she would have.

Epilogue

Eighteen Months Later

Joseph took the parcel from Jimmy, closed the library door, and walked over to where Meadow was pacing in front of the large window. As he approached, she whirled around, nearly barreling into Laurie. The latter steadied Meadow as she blurted, "Is that it?"

He held out the brown paper-wrapped package. "Either that, or someone wants to add to your library."

She took the book, and it was a sign of her nervousness that she didn't tease him back. As she unwrapped it, Laurie massaged her neck, and Joseph wrapped an arm about her waist.

In her hands was a leather-bound book emblazoned

with gold letters that read, *Discover the Dawn* by E. Meadows.

Which was the pen name she'd chosen to use.

She traced the letters. "I still can't believe it's real."

Laurie laid his head atop hers. "You worked hard on this book, Emmy. And it's good, damn good, to the point I couldn't put it down. Everyone will want a copy, just wait and see."

A tear trailed down her cheek, and Joseph rubbed it away with his thumb. "Laurie's still standing and isn't in crippling pain, so you know it's the truth."

"I know. But it's just so hard to believe. Once I got my powers and my father made plans, I never thought I'd get the chance."

He took the book, placed it on a side table, and wrapped his arms around both Meadow and Laurie. "Between this and how in-demand you are at Nyx's Kingdom, you've accomplished so much, love. I wonder what's next. The Fae Witch Council?"

She scrunched her nose. "No way. Besides, my pen name is a loosely kept secret, and this story alone will disqualify me, especially since I want to write another one. Although…"

He leaned back and asked, "Although, what?"

She glanced at Laurie and then at him. "Maybe it's time to try and give Eloise a cousin."

Eloise was River and Nora's daughter. She was beloved by all, and even had her vampire Dark Lord uncle wrapped around her little finger.

For a second, joy shot through Joseph at the thought of being a father. But then he remembered the last time they'd discussed this, and it hadn't gone well. "Have you changed your mind?"

She gently pushed against them and stood back so she could look at both him and Laurie. "No. I understand where you're coming from, but I want fate to decide the father of our child."

Joseph had argued it would be easier if Laurie fathered their children, and then they wouldn't have to face discrimination and abuse from any humans they encountered. However, Meadow didn't want to give the small-minded bastards such power over their future family.

Laurie walked up to him, placed a hand on his jaw, and gently turned his head to look at him. He caressed Joseph's face as he said, "I understand where you're coming from, but you know I agree with Meadow. No matter whether you or I father the child, they will be *our* child. All of ours. And who knows, maybe we'll both father children and then that'll really get the human prudes talking. Wouldn't that be something?"

Laurie winked, and Joseph's lips twitched. "I'm sure we get them talking already. Between our pleasure house expansions into the shifter and fae witch territories, and our triad marriage, we're not exactly conforming with Victorian human expectations."

Meadow joined them and touched his upper arm. "So why stop there? They'll probably just be jealous. I mean, it's like a baby surprise, isn't it? Without DNA testing and all that future stuff, we won't know until the birth itself. And by that point, I'll just be happy to not be pregnant any longer, given what I saw with Nora.

And once he or she arrives, will you act differently if you or Laurie are the sperm donor?"

"Of course not."

She smiled. "There you go." She moved to stand between Laurie and Joseph, and they instantly wrapped their arms around each other. "Maybe we should get started right now. If we conceive while celebrating the release of my book, then that would be an amazing story to tell one day."

He snorted. "You're not going to write our child's conception story into a book."

Laurie grinned. "I rather like the idea. Especially if we end up with twins or triplets. Babies from both of us? Now, wouldn't that be something?"

"Don't even joke about that, Laurie Yates. You're going to tempt fate, and I'll end up the size of a small barge."

Laurie kissed her gently. "A beautiful barge."

She playfully hit his chest, and Joseph laughed.

As Laurie and Meadow continued bantering, he merely held his wife and husband and pictured them together in the future, except then Meadow was holding their baby.

And in that moment, he didn't care who ended up the father. If Meadow and Laurie wanted fate to decide, then he would, too.

Because Meadow was right—his suggesting otherwise gave the small-minded arseholes the win.

In the middle of their bantering, he scooped Meadow into his arms, and she squeaked as she wrapped her arms around his neck. Joseph glanced at

Laurie and asked, "Ready to celebrate and start that conception story?"

Laurie grinned, took off the ring that prevented him from getting anyone pregnant, and then did the same with Joseph's. "Now we are."

He carried Meadow into the bedroom, with Laurie at his side, and then proceeded to cherish both his husband and wife.

And as they laughed and moaned and held each other close, Joseph reveled in his life full of love and belonging, and looked forward to growing old with Meadow, Laurie, and any children they might have.

Author's Note

If you're here reading this note, thank you! I know there was a long stretch between the release of the third and fourth books. This was mostly a mistake on my part to try and follow trends with a pen name that didn't work out. I've learned to stick to writing what I enjoy most instead of trying to write to what people are asking for. (You think I'd have learned this lesson already…but sometimes we all get distracted by shiny things, haha.) Jumping back into this world meant re-reading the first three books, and now that I have ALL my notes and character details, the rest of the series should be a lot easier to write!

Speaking of which, the next one will be about William Khan and Grace Black (if you couldn't tell) and will be called *Wolf's Fae Witch Lord*. My goal is to release it at the end of this year (2026) or January 2027 at the latest. I'm excited to finally see the aloof fae witch Dark Lord fall for the (mostly) blind wolf-shifter female and finally learn to trust and soften around her. :)

As for Laurie, Joseph, and Meadow's story, it was definitely a challenge for me. I've never written a story where three people all fall in love with each other, and I was actually nervous to start. However, the more I got to know them all, the easier the story became. And if you're wondering about the fae witches using dark arts…that will be handled in Khan's story! He has some work to do…

As always, I have a lot of people who helped me along the way. I'd like to thank:

- My betas: Iliana, Sabrina, Ashley, and Amy. They catch lingering typos and spot minor inconsistencies, and these ladies are truly amazing.
- My readers and fans. You were not only patient for this story, you all make my dream job possible, and I couldn't do it without you!

Thanks again for reading and I can't wait to share William and Grace's story in *Wolf's Fae Witch Lord.* I'll see you at the end of the next book!

Also by Jessie Donovan

Dark Lords of London

Vampire's Modern Bride (DLL #1)

Vampire's Fae Witch Healer (DLL #2)

Fae Witch's Vampire Guard (DLL #3)

Vampires' Shared Bride (DLL #4)

Wolf's Fae Witch Lord / Grace & Khan (DLL #5 / Late 2026 or early 2027)

Dragon Clan Gatherings

Summer at Lochguard (DCG #1)

Winter at Stonefire (DCG #2)

Kelderan Runic Warriors

The Conquest (KRW #1)

The Barren (KRW #2)

The Heir (KRW #3)

The Forbidden (KRW #4)

The Hidden (KRW #5)

The Survivor (KRW #6)

Lochguard Highland Dragons

The Dragon's Dilemma (LHD #1)

The Dragon Guardian (LHD #2)

The Dragon's Heart (LHD #3)

The Dragon Warrior (LHD #4)

The Dragon Family (LHD #5)

The Dragon's Discovery (LHD #6)

The Dragon's Pursuit (LHD #7)

The Dragon Collective (LHD #8)

The Dragon's Chance (LHD # 9)

The Dragon's Memory (LHD #10)

The Dragon Recruit (LHD #11)

Mariana Barlow & Brodie MacNeil / Late 2026 (LHD #12)

Stonefire Dragons

Sacrificed to the Dragon (SD #1)

Seducing the Dragon (SD #2)

Revealing the Dragons (SD #3)

Healed by the Dragon (SD #4)

Reawakening the Dragon (SD #5)

Loved by the Dragon (SD #6)

Surrendering to the Dragon (SD #7)

Cured by the Dragon (SD #8)

Aiding the Dragon (SD #9)

Finding the Dragon (SD #10)

Craved by the Dragon (SD #11)

Persuading the Dragon (SD #12)

Treasured by the Dragon (SD #13)

Trusting the Dragon (SD #14)

Taught by the Dragon (SD #15)

Charming the Dragon (SD #16)

Claimed by the Dragon (SD #17)

Stonefire Dragons Shorts

Meeting the Humans (SDS #1)

The Dragon Camp (SDS #2)

The Dragon Play (SDS #3)

Dragon's First Christmas (SDS #4)

The Dragon's Treasure (SDS #5)

Stonefire Dragons Universe

Winning Skyhunter (SDU #1)

Transforming Snowridge (SDU #2)

Finding Dragon's Court (SDU #3)

Masked Dragon of Snowridge (SDU #4)

Protecting Seahaven / Dr. Emily Davies & Cam Alexander / Summer 2026 (SDU #5)

Tahoe Dragon Mates

The Dragon's Choice (TDM #1)

The Dragon's Need (TDM #2)

The Dragon's Bidder (TDM #3)

The Dragon's Charge (TDM #4)

The Dragon's Weakness (TDM #5)

The Dragon's Find (TDM #6)

The Dragon's Surprise (TDM #7)

Asylums for Magical Threats

Blaze of Secrets (AMT #1)

Frozen Desires (AMT #2)

Shadow of Temptation (AMT #3)

Flare of Promise (AMT #4)

Cascade Shifters

Convincing the Cougar (CS #0.5)

Reclaiming the Wolf (CS #1)

Cougar's First Christmas (CS #2)

Resisting the Cougar (CS #3)

Love in Scotland

Crazy Scottish Love (LiS #1)

Chaotic Scottish Wedding (LiS #2)

WRITING AS KAYLA CHASE

(Sexy contemporary romances)

Starry Hills

Want Me Forever

Stay With Me Forever

Marry Me Forever

Trust Me With Forever

About the Author

Jessie Donovan has sold over half a million books, has given away hundreds of thousands more to readers for free, and has even hit the *NY Times* and *USA Today* bestseller lists. She is best known for her dragon-shifter series, but also writes about vampires, fae witches, aliens, and even has a crazy romantic comedy series set in Scotland. When not reading a book, jogging on her treadmill, or traipsing around some foreign country on a shoestring, she can often be found interacting with her readers on Facebook or TikTok. She lives near Seattle, where, yes, it rains a lot but it also makes everything green.

Visit her website at: www.JessieDonovan.com

www.ingramcontent.com/pod-product-compliance
Lightning Source LLC
LaVergne TN
LVHW090556110826
845146LV00001B/143

* 9 7 9 8 8 9 1 5 6 1 0 0 7 *